A LIZ ADAMS MYSTERY

CARMEL CONUNDRUM

*To Kathy —
Hope you enjoy!
Stacy Wilder*

STACY WILDER

This is a work of fiction. Names, characters, places, and incidents either are the product of the author's imagination or are used fictitiously. Any resemblance to actual persons, living or dead, events, or locales is entirely coincidental.

Copyright © 2022 by Stacy Wilder

All rights reserved. No part of this book may be reproduced or used in any manner without written permission of the copyright owner except for the use of quotations in a book review.

Cover design by Brandi Doane McCann

Interior design by Laura Doyle

ISBN 979-8-9854266-2-5 (paperback)

ISBN 979-8-9854266-3-2 (ebook)

www.storystacy.com

Prologue

Partially obscured behind gray-tinged clouds, the crimson moon glowed. Incense burned and released the scent of sandalwood and sage. A gust of wind intensified the evening chill. Apollo adjusted his magenta-colored robe and took his place at the outdoor wooden altar. "My new friends, I regret that you have decided to leave our haven. Before you go tonight, we will break bread together."

Apollo slipped on latex gloves and lifted the silver goblet overhead. "May our homeless friends find great prosperity when they return from whence they came." He lowered the vessel and took a deep sip. He picked up a loaf of bread, broke it into bits, and placed the pieces on the silver platter. "May this food nourish your souls and give you sustenance on the journey ahead of you." He bowed his head. "Amen."

The two men and the young woman who stood in front of the altar nodded and repeated, "Amen." Freshly showered and dressed in new clothes, they were eager to return to the lifestyle they knew. The other seven homeless people who'd originally arrived with them on the bus had decided to stay. The facility offered food, shelter, and steady work.

One of Apollo's wives passed the plate of bread around. She also wore gloves. Apollo stepped down from the altar. He took off his purple robe and handed it to wife number two. "Let's proceed."

As they boarded the van, wife number three provided each of them with a brown paper bag. The sack contained a sandwich, a brownie, chips, and a bottle of water.

Apollo sat stoically in the passenger seat. From years of experience, he'd learned the initial poison didn't always take. Tucked in his left jacket pocket were syringes loaded with extra. Just in case. He was always amazed when someone decided not to remain on the compound.

Soon they would arrive at the coastal tree-lined property where he and his parents once lived. As he recalled the makeshift tent they'd called home, he shuddered. Born Ed Lester to homeless parents, Apollo had been astounded when they passed away, and he discovered they were quite wealthy. He couldn't understand why anyone would choose a homeless lifestyle voluntarily.

When he had recreated himself as Apollo, he'd attempted unsuccessfully to acquire the property. Instead, he'd purchased more affordable land nearby and began building Mission Apollo with his inheritance. The compound now included a chapel, the main office, two long barracks, a school, a sick bay, and a dining hall. The addition of a third barrack was in progress. Since the Mission's inception, the population had grown to nearly one hundred women, men, and children.

Anointed by God, he was carrying out God's mission to get the homeless off the streets. As Apollo brushed his long wavy black curls off his shoulder, he imagined the satisfaction he'd experience tomorrow when he'd return to the sacred ground to offer a final blessing.

CARMEL CONUNDRUM

The van driver drove in silence to the uninhabited piece of land where the three who chose not to stay would find their eternal home.

Chapter 1

A cool breeze greeted us as Duke and I stepped off the private jet and walked across the tarmac. I could definitely get used to this lifestyle. The flight had been smooth, the steward attentive and friendly. Brad had thought of all the details, including rawhides on the plane for my dog and a lobster lunch for me. Duke, my six-year-old black Labrador, had curled next to my seat and acted as if he'd flown private all his life.

We climbed into a waiting limousine. I was both nervous and excited to see Brad. In a letter each of us received after her death a few months ago, our mutual friend, Peg, had encouraged both of us to stay in touch. I was here to visit him, check out a piece of property she'd left me, and take a break from the PI business. Once things had settled down after Peg's murder, Brad and I had planned this trip, and we'd been communicating daily. My heart ached over the loss of my best friend, and I was still recovering from trying to solve her murder and being accused of it at the same time. The pain of the loss lessened as I shared the grief with Peg's childhood friend, Brad, and her business partner and dear friend, Lou.

I wasn't sure what category Brad fell into for me. Certainly friend. Possibly lover. Maybe more. Before I'd left Charleston, I had changed traveling outfits three times, eventually deciding on a simple white peasant blouse, jeans, and a pair of sexy sling-back sandals. So far, Brad and I had only exchanged a kiss—and oh, that kiss—and some suggestive phone conversations.

Today, Brad had a business meeting he couldn't reschedule so he'd sent the car instead. Duke, oblivious to my nerves, hung his head out the limousine window. His tongue flopped while his nose wiggled, taking in the smells of California. The cool, dry breeze was refreshing. What a change in climate from Charleston.

As we turned into the driveway, my eyes grew wide. The sprawling, gray stone two-story home set against the backdrop of the Pacific Ocean had to be worth a mint. A Southern-style wrap-around driftwood porch framed the front. I spotted Brad sitting in an Adirondack chair. He sported an untucked white polo and navy shorts. The white contrasted with his golden California tan. When we pulled to the front of the circular driveway, he quickly rose and sprinted down the stairs.

"Sorry I couldn't meet you at the airport."

I felt disappointed when he gave me a rather chaste kiss, then grabbed Duke's leash and lavished love on my dog. The limo driver placed my luggage inside the house, and Brad sent him on his way. "I'll take him for a quick walk, so he can do his business. Go on in and make yourself at home. The powder room is on the left, right off the entry."

I walked inside and admired the view. Sprawling glass windows showcased the Pacific Ocean. Today the waves were choppy. The sun drifted in and out of long white clouds, casting shadows on the water. Further back from the house were a massive outdoor kitchen and an infinity pool. Nice.

As soon as I finished freshening up, Brad walked in, and my heart did a flip-flop.

He reached for me, wrapped me in those well-toned arms, and kissed me slow, tender, and deep. Nothing chaste about this kiss. Boldly, I slipped my hands underneath his shirt, relishing the warmth of his smooth skin. Ignorant of the heat building between the two of us, Duke curled up by the fireplace and settled in for a nap. I stepped back before things spiraled out of hand. Brad sighed and ran his fingers through his hair. "Let me show you your room so you can get settled."

The guest bedroom was decorated in shades of gray accented with pops of aquamarine. The bed stacked with pillows beckoned. I covered a yawn with my hand.

"Why don't you take a nap? I bet you're exhausted."

"Actually, that sounds divine. You don't mind?"

He gave me another long kiss as an answer. "Sweet dreams."

Two hours later, I awakened. As I emerged from under the covers, I surveyed my new surroundings. The artwork was a bit modern for my taste, abstracts with splashes of identical hues of gray and blue. Several remotes sat on the bedside table. I picked up the one labeled 'Window Shades.' Once I'd raised them, I was greeted with an incredible view of the ocean. Blinded by the sunlight, I lowered them back down and picked up the TV remote. I hadn't noticed a TV in the room. When I pressed the 'on' button, a painting that hung over a long dresser, where my luggage sat, morphed into images of a baseball game in progress. Way cool.

I climbed out of bed, pulled my cosmetic case out of my suitcase, and headed for the bathroom to brush my teeth. An oversized whirlpool tub sat on a dark gray slate floor. The counter tops were light gray granite. I admired the impressionistic-style oil paintings of the Pacific coast perfectly arranged on the walls. Peg had been a high-end decorator before she passed, and I recognized her influence in every inch of this space. I was both comforted and saddened by the sight.

After I freshened up, I searched for Duke and Brad. I found Brad in the kitchen chopping vegetables as he listened to the Eagles' "Hotel California." Duke was curled at his feet. "How'd you sleep?"

"Great. I can't believe I slept for two hours."

"You probably needed it. I'm so glad you're here." He set down the knife and walked over and kissed me. I suddenly felt awkward and a bit shy. When Duke finally realized I was in the room, he wriggled toward me, tail wagging. I nodded at the chopped veggies. "Um, can I help?"

"Sure. Pick a bottle from the wine fridge in the pantry. I thought we'd eat here tonight. I'm grilling steaks." After perusing the wine selection, I chose a shiraz, twisted the cap off, and poured each of us a glass. "Did Peg help you decorate this place? Your home is gorgeous."

"Of course she did. You think I could do this?" He pointed at himself and smirked.

We were interrupted by the buzz of his phone. Brad glanced at the name on the screen. "Sorry. I've got to take this call."

Since we were in the same room, I couldn't help but overhear Brad's side of the conversation. "Hey, Tim, what's up? No way. Who is it this time?" He paused a moment to listen, then said, "We need to get to the bottom of this. Soon. Before word gets out and our reputation is destroyed." He glanced over at me and said, "I have an idea. Check my calendar and book a meeting for Monday, preferably morning. We can discuss what I have in mind then." Brad turned back toward me. "I have a business proposition for you."

"What is it?"

"Why don't you change into your swimsuit? You can relax in the pool while I grill the steaks. I'll explain then."

~ * ~

I felt self-conscious in my bikini. My workout routine had been spotty since Peg's death. The chocolate eclairs I'd consumed in

Paris while investigating Peg's murder hadn't helped my waistline. Plus, I was hanging out with Mr. Triathlete. I slipped on a matching coral cover-up and joined Brad outside. "What can I do?"

Brad placed the meat on the hot grill. "Nothing, I've got this." While the steaks sizzled, he sat on a lounge chair next to the pool. "I forgot to ask. How was the flight?"

"Great. Thank you for the lobster." I swiftly shed my cover-up and joined Duke in the pool. He was having a grand time swimming to and from the steps. As the music flowed through the outdoor speakers, I began to relax.

"You're welcome. Nice swimsuit."

"Thanks." My face grew warm. "I could definitely get used to flying private. I'm envious."

While the sun slowly set in the background, casting hues of pink and purple on the water, I hung onto the side of the pool and admired the view. Brad wore turquoise swim trunks and no shirt.

He picked at the fabric on the chair. A minute of silence passed before he responded, "It took me a long time to get on a plane after what happened to my parents."

"I'm sorry." I wished I could take back my earlier comment. His parents had perished on Flight 93 on 9/11.

He stood to check the grill. With his back toward me, he continued, "For the longest time, I avoided planes, taking the train, bus, or driving—whatever got me there the fastest."

I had to strain my ears to catch the words. I watched as Brad placed foil-wrapped corn next to the steaks.

"When the company finally took off, I invested in a private jet. Peg joined me on the first flight. I almost didn't get on the plane."

Although Peg and I'd been best friends since I'd moved to Charleston six years ago, Brad had been friends with her since childhood. "I can't imagine what that was like for you."

His shoulders slumped. "Yeah, I still have my moments, but I manage. I thoroughly vet the pilot, steward, and crew for every flight. I wouldn't have put you and Duke on the plane otherwise." He placed the tongs on the granite counter top of the outdoor kitchen and changed the subject. "About the earlier phone call, I shouldn't have said anything. You're supposed to be here relaxing. I wasn't thinking." He stared at the smoke rising from the grill.

I stepped out of the pool and wrapped a towel around my torso. I placed my arm across his shoulder and asked, "What's going on?" If there were problems with his business, he hadn't mentioned anything during our phone calls.

"Four of our former clients have had their identities stolen. This will ruin MultiPoint if I don't stop it soon." He ran his fingers through his hair.

Wow. I knew how much his company meant to him. When his parents passed, he'd fallen into a deep depression. With Peg's help, he'd pulled himself out of the slump, finished college, and started MultiPoint Protection Services. Part of Brad's high-tech company involved protecting people's information. The news of stolen identities didn't bode well. "Former clients? How long has this been going on?" I added.

"We recently discovered the thefts. Every one of the victims died within the last year and someone canceled their service."

I moved to a nearby lounge chair so I could see his face. "Were you hacked?"

"I don't see how," he frowned. "Anyway, it was selfish to ask you to work on your vacation. Let's forget about it and enjoy dinner."

I was intrigued. "Identity theft is not really my area of expertise. I could ask around and find someone for you." As I rubbed my chin, I contemplated the situation. "Why don't I go into the office with you and meet with Tim? I can take a look at what you have. It might give me some ideas."

A slow smile lit up his face. "You'd do that?"

"Of course. I want to help." One day wasn't going to hurt. Besides, maybe I'd sell my newly acquired property, get rich, buy my own private plane, and take a permanent vacation from sleuthing.

He walked over and kissed my cheek. "Thank you." He stepped back, gazed into my eyes for a few moments and then turned his attention back toward the grill. "By the way, the office is pet friendly. You're welcome to bring Duke."

At the sound of his name, he emerged from the pool, shaking water in all directions.

Brad laughed and grabbed a towel. "C'mon boy, let's dry you off." I joined him and attempted to corral my wiggly dog. As we toweled him off, we bumped noses. Brad reached for my face, traced his finger along my jaw, and then kissed my lips. I shivered from both the kiss and the cooling temperatures. An evening fog had begun to roll in. I dropped the towel on a patio chair, picked up my cover-up, and pulled it over my head.

Brad put on a long sleeve shirt and then switched on the outdoor heaters. Nearby a glass-top table was set with candles and wine. A few minutes later, he plated the food, and we ate our steak dinner by candlelight. He set a small plate on the ground with bits of meat for Duke. My heart skipped a beat as his tail swished through the air in delight.

I picked up the corncob and inhaled the scent of garlic-infused butter. As I bit into the grilled corn, I closed my eyes and savored the juicy flavors. "This is delicious."

"I'm not too good in the kitchen, but I do OK with the grill. Tomorrow, we'll go visit the property and then go into town. You can do a little shopping, and we can celebrate Peg's birthday at her favorite Carmel restaurant."

I set the half-eaten corncob back on my plate. My heart sank.

Tomorrow.

What would have been Peg's thirty-seventh birthday. Last year, Peg and I spent her birthday at the beach. After a day of sun and water, we'd returned, cleaned up, and hit the nightspots in downtown Charleston. Our neighbor, friend, and Peg's business partner, Lou, had joined us. We didn't get home until two a.m.

As Billy Joel crooned "Only the Good Die Young" through the outdoor speakers, Brad reached across the table and grabbed my hand. "You OK?"

I dabbed at the corner of my eye with a napkin. "Yeah, that sounds fine. I was remembering celebrating with her last year. The firsts are always the toughest, aren't they?"

The first birthday celebration without her.

Tears streamed down my cheeks as we held hands and listened to the lyrics. When the song finished, he wiped my tears away, his fingers lingering on my face longer than necessary. Duke whined and broke the trance.

"Life won't be the same without her," I said.

We began reminiscing about birthdays and holidays spent with Peg. As I mopped up the last bit of garlic butter with a slice of French bread, I complimented Brad's grilling skills. "Thank you. Dinner was wonderful." I stood to clear the plates.

Brad waved his hands. "Leave them. I have a better idea. It's a beautiful night. Why don't we relax in the hot tub? I'll refill our wine glasses."

The fresh pang of pain from sharing Peg stories sat heavy in my chest. I begged off, claiming I was exhausted.

He frowned and then agreed, "You're right. It's been a long day, and we have a big day ahead of us tomorrow." He stood, shut off the outdoor heaters, and picked up a remote.

I watched as an automated cover moved over the pool. "Fancy."

"Safety measure." He gathered up the empty plates, opened the back door, and went inside.

Puzzled by his clipped response, I wondered if the extra precaution had anything to do with his sister's childhood drowning accident. I cleared the rest of dinner off the table and joined him in the kitchen. He'd already started washing the dishes. I opened the dishwasher and prepared to help him.

"No, no. You need your beauty sleep." He winked.

"The cook is not supposed to clean," I protested.

He wiped his hands on the dishtowel, turned toward me, and kissed me long and slow. "Goodnight, Liz. I'll see you in the morning."

Tucked away safely with Duke in the bedroom, I wondered what tomorrow would bring. Brad's kisses touched me to the core. Where would this go next?

Wherever it was going, was I ready?

Chapter 2

As Apollo walked to the communal dining room, he reflected on the previous evening's events. Everything had gone as planned. After he'd confirmed each person had succumbed to the poison, he and his Disciples had lovingly placed each body in a shroud. Sprinkling dried herbs on the corpses, they'd wrapped the bodies in the sacred cloth and carried them along the beach to a cavern. Once inside, they'd switched on their lanterns and navigated the narrow passageway to a large opening. As they chanted "Om," they'd laid the bodies on top of the others.

"My dearly departed new friends," Apollo's voice had echoed in the confined space. "You will never be hungry or thirsty again." He'd paused, lifted his face to the ceiling, and raised his arms high. "You will always have a roof over your head." When he returned his hands to his heart, he bowed his head. "May you rest in peace in your sacred home."

His Disciples had replied, "Amen."

Apollo then led the group in prayer. Afterward, they'd exited the cavern in silence.

He returned to the present and smiled. Before he entered the dining room, he checked his appearance in the small mirror he kept in his pants pocket. Once his morning duties were complete, he'd drive solo to the property to give his final blessing. The incense was already prepared. He rubbed his hands together in anticipation of his visit to the sacred ground where he'd once lived, and where both his parents were buried.

The early sunlight streamed through the thin curtains as the Members made their way through the buffet line. Long wooden tables with benches lined the space. Once everyone was seated, Apollo led the group in prayer. A key Disciple perused the sign-in list and counted heads. The children sat together at a separate table. After breakfast, they'd follow their teachers to the on-site school. As he walked from table to table, Apollo greeted each Member by name and wished them a blessed and productive day.

In less than an hour, the adults would report to their respective jobs on campus, whether it be teaching, tending to the garden and animals, building the newest quarters, cooking, cleaning, running the operations, providing security, or working in the underground drug warehouse. They would reconvene for lunch at high noon and then return to work. Afterward, they'd gather for dinner and then proceed to the chapel for worship before settling in for the night. A mild sedative in the communal wine would guarantee a peaceful night for all.

The man who'd arrived on the latest bus, Peanut, didn't like it here one bit. Peanut had earned his nickname in the Army for his size and his ability to squeeze through small spaces. He couldn't remember the last time anyone had called him by his real name, Jim. He wished that he'd left with his friend, Rumor. They'd met two years ago, and she was like a daughter to him. He wondered if she was OK.

When Apollo had touted the benefits of life on the compound and asked if they wanted to make a lifetime commitment, he'd said yes, confident he'd be able to change his mind. A break from the streets sounded great. After two days, he was ready to leave. Rumor had made the better decision.

The food was good enough. Today's breakfast of scrambled eggs, bacon, biscuits, and fresh fruit was the best he'd had since his wife had died of cancer ten years ago, and he'd started taking drugs. The free dope here was a bonus . . . but they hardly got a spare moment to themselves, and that Apollo dude walked around like his shit didn't stink. Plus, he had like a gazillion so-called wives. Something was off, but Peanut couldn't figure it out. The Disciples watched over the place like it was some kind of prison. He'd escaped from a jail in Mexico. He could bust out of this place, too.

Peanut placed his empty plate, glass, and silverware in the dish-washing bins and followed the Newbies, the most recent recruits, outside. Once they'd completed their training, they'd earn the title of Member. Over time, the more ambitious Members could become Disciples and be a part of Apollo's inner circle.

Peanut rolled his eyes at the two dudes at the front of the pack who followed Disciple Cosmo like puppies. He adjusted his name tag on the Mission provided lime-colored t-shirt.

All the so-called Disciples had weird names, and Apollo's wives were sometimes referred to by the number tattooed on their right wrist. Today, the Newbies would continue the tour of the facility, learning about each area and the jobs they could perform. Peanut had already decided. He wanted to work in the garden. It was his best chance to case the place for a way out.

A job in security wasn't a choice. He'd have to be here a year to be eligible for that gig. At least he'd be able to 'apply' for the position that he wanted. He felt confident he'd get it. He couldn't see any of the yahoos in his group enjoying digging in the dirt. Yup. It was only a matter of time before he'd be out of here.

Chapter 3

Brad rapped at my bedroom door. "Wake up, Sunshine. Coffee's ready."

I stretched my limbs underneath the bedspread and replied, "Be out in a bit." I was still getting used to the time change. Duke hopped off the bed and whined at the door.

"OK if I take him out?" He cracked the door open.

I pulled up the covers to hide my make-up-free face. "Sure."

My dog scurried out the door. "You'll want to dress warm. It can get chilly on the coast."

Half an hour later I emerged from the bedroom barefoot, dressed in a black turtleneck and jeans. Brad kissed me on the cheek. "Hmm, you're wearing my favorite perfume, Amazing Grace." He tugged on my blonde ponytail. Duke was eating his breakfast. I fidgeted with my earring, unsettled by the new surroundings and the idea of Brad tending to my dog. Duke appeared unfazed.

"How do you like your coffee?"

His coffee machine looked like something used on a spaceship. I imagined the instructions were as long as a full-length novel.

"Um, honestly, normally I'm a tea drinker, but coffee sounds better. Milk and sugar, please." My stomach quivered as I watched him.

"I have all kinds of tea, too." He pointed to the pantry as he warmed the milk. After stirring in a generous teaspoon of sugar, he handed me the mug. I inhaled the scent. "Smells wonderful."

Brad had laid out fruit, bagels, butter, and several types of jellies on the kitchen island. "I'm not big on breakfast. I'd be happy to make you a protein shake if you'd like."

I imagined he'd already gone on his run and swam a few laps in the pool. "No, this is perfect." I popped half a bagel into the toaster.

"Peg's property is about a twenty-minute drive from here. We'll set off in about an hour. Let the fog lift a bit."

"Can Duke come along?" I slathered butter and cherry jelly on the bread.

"Of course. We'll need to keep him on a leash. It's a big piece of property, and we wouldn't want him to tangle with a mountain lion."

My mouth dropped open. "Yikes. Maybe we should leave him behind."

"Don't worry. It's rare to see them, and I have an air horn I'll bring, just in case. You might want to wear something brighter, though."

"My wind jacket is orange."

"That'll work." Brad rinsed out his mug and placed it in the dishwasher. "After we take a look at the property, we can grab some lunch along the coast. And then we can drop Duke back at the house, change, and head to Carmel to do a little shopping before dinner."

I consumed the last of the bagel. "Sounds like a plan."

～ * ～

Sunlight beamed from a baby blue sky burning off the morning fog. I hoped Brad didn't mind the slobber splattering his Range Rover as Duke hung his head out the back window. As he navigated the curves in the road faster than I preferred, I couldn't tear my eyes away from the wild, rugged coastline. Cliffs dropped to sandy beaches. Waves lapped against rocks. I mouthed a wow as a red-tailed hawk soared overhead.

"Stunning, isn't it?"

"It's fantastic, so different from the dunes and sea oats of the Carolina coast."

"Wait until you see your property. We're almost there."

A few more minutes of silence passed before Brad signaled a turn with his blinker. He pulled onto a dirt road lined with pine trees and drove another mile.

"This is it." After he put the car in park, he hopped out and punched in the code to open the steel gate connected to the worn wooden fence surrounding the property. He climbed back into the Rover and we continued down the bumpy path. "We'll drive until the road runs out and then take the trail down to the coastline. You might want to replace the fence. It doesn't offer much protection from unwanted visitors."

The temperature dropped slightly as we drove down the dirt track. Pine trees, cypresses, and oaks stretched textured trunks and branches toward the sky. My eyes wandered over the ferns and foliage in shades of green from pale lime to deep hunter. Finally, the view opened into a magnificent clearing. Brad parked the car. I let Duke out and snapped on his leash.

Wildflowers in yellows, pinks, and purples bloomed profusely. Butterflies darted from flower to flower. The scenery resembled an impressionist painting. I couldn't believe this was mine. A single picnic table and a porta-potty tucked behind a group of trees were the only signs of civilization.

I recalled the payment I made for last month's bill. "Why did Peg have a porta-potty?"

"Maybe she wanted the convenience when she visited? Or, knowing Peg, she did it for the landscaping crew."

Last week, I'd received the quarterly invoice from the company that cleared fallen limbs and kept the road free of debris.

"C'mon. I want to show you something."

My heart fluttered when Brad grabbed my hand and led me to a dirt trail.

"It's about half a mile to the coastline. The path is a little rough. You'll be glad you wore those shoes."

My hiking boots were brand new and weren't my usual fashion statement, but I was grateful for them as we navigated the rugged terrain. Duke marked his territory along the way. Suddenly, Brad put his arm in front of me, halting my progress.

"Shh," he whispered and pointed ahead.

When I spotted the mountain lion perched on a rock fifty yards down the path, my heart hammered in my ears. My whole body tensed. I yanked the leash tighter to my body and hoped that Duke didn't spot the animal as his nose twitched at the smell in the breeze. Brad pulled the air horn out of his pocket and prepared to sound it if needed. The tawny feline's paws were huge. I held my breath, trying to make as little noise as possible. As soon as the creature spotted us, Brad sounded the horn and the animal's muscular body darted off into the trees. Duke barked, and I took in a deep gulp of air while gripping the leash tighter so Duke wouldn't chase the big cat.

"That's lucky."

After I'd released my breath, I said, "Lucky?"

"Yeah, you got to see a mountain lion. How cool is that? Probably a male. He was a decent size."

"Let's go back." I was glad that I relieved my bladder before we left the house. Duke sensed my unease and whined.

"Trust me. That mountain lion is long gone. He's way more scared of us." Brad grabbed my hand. "Come on. You have to see your beach."

His enthusiasm was contagious, and I reluctantly followed him down the path while hanging on to his hand. My heart rate slowed as I diligently searched the brush for any lingering cats. Once I'd calmed down, I had to agree with Brad. Seeing the creature was definitely cool.

My mind returned to my current dilemma about the property. "Do you know what Peg planned to do with the land?"

"A couple of real estate agents approached her. She didn't think the time was right to sell. I know one of them. I'll give you his name."

We slowly made our way down the rocky trail that led to the beach, and the path eventually opened up to the Pacific. Seagulls soared overhead. A pelican dove into the water for a fish. A bob of seals sunned themselves on the rocks offshore. A raft of sea otters drifted in the ocean. Duke jerked on his leash and tugged me toward the water.

"Wait." Brad grabbed Duke's lead to stop him and kissed me. "Had to christen your first visit."

Giving way to my dog's tugs, we walked to the shoreline and then let Duke off-leash. Brad laughed as my dog ran to the beach and leaped at the surf, dolphining his nose in and out of the water.

"He's going to be a mess," I shook my head.

"That's why I brought towels."

My heart melted at the discovery that this man couldn't care less if Duke got sand and saltwater all over his expensive car. While we walked hand-in-hand along the shore, I gasped as a humpback whale breached the surface of the sea in a spectacular splash. I surveyed the landscape and noticed a figure looming in the distance.

"Is that part of my land?"

"Yeah, I don't know what that guy's doing here. Let's check it out."

The man stood at the entrance of what appeared to be a cavern. He had a backpack in his hand. As we approached, I detected an odd smell. Incense? He was dressed in a V-neck white linen shirt and black pants. Sand coated his black sneakers.

Brad waved a hello. Duke began to growl. "Excuse me, sir. Did you know this is private property?"

"No. Sorry. Had no clue." His deep voice boomed like a television preacher. After he spoke, Duke yipped. Someone once told me that all dogs have superpowers. Duke's was communication. He whined when something was up. He yipped when someone wasn't telling the truth. I'd discovered his talents when he was a year old. After I'd put him through rigorous tests, I'd determined he was more reliable than a lie detector. I wondered why this guy was lying.

"Well, this is Liz Adams, the property owner. I'm Brad O'Connor." He extended his hand. "And you are?"

The man got a quizzical look on his face. He was over six feet tall and broad-shouldered. The wind blew his long, curly black hair off his shoulders. Framed by long black lashes, his eyes were a piercing blue. He paused for a moment then offered his hand in return. "Apollo. Pleased to meet you."

Duke's hackles were up, and I had chill bumps on my arms despite the sun's warm rays.

"I'll be on my way. Was just enjoying this beautiful day. Had no idea this was private."

The comment earned another yip, followed by a low growl.

"How'd you get here?" Brad wasn't letting him off that lightly.

"Car's parked up the road. Nice to meet you folks. Have a good day." He quickly slung the pack over his shoulders and took off in the opposite direction before either of us could ask another question.

"Watch out for mountain lions," Brad muttered under his breath.

~ * ~

Fortunately, we'd evaded any mountain lion encounters on our way back to the car. I brushed the sand off the bottom of my jeans. My stomach rumbled as I climbed into the Rover.

"Sounds like you're hungry."

"I'm famished." I guess running into massive cats can do that to you.

"I think you'll like the lunch spot I picked. The views of the Pacific are amazing, and the menu has everything from seafood to hamburgers." Duke let out a woof from the back seat.

As he put the car into reverse, he commented, "You know something about that guy is familiar. But I can't quite place him."

"He gave me the creeps. Plus, he's way too pretty for a man."

"Too pretty?"

"Never mind." I waved the comment off. "What an odd name, Apollo."

Brad jerked his head upright. "I remember now. There was a feature article about him in the paper last year. He has some kind of compound not too far from here. Mission Apollo. He's all about saving the homeless. His team takes buses into cities in the surrounding areas. They offer them a fresh start, giving them a room and free meals in exchange for working jobs on the compound."

"Sounds kind of like a cult." I turned toward Brad. "Did Peg know about them?" When Peg was alive, she had a foundation that supported causes that helped homeless people and homeless pets. Her niece, Jenny, was in charge of the foundation now.

"I scanned the article and sent it to her. She wanted to find out more." We sat in silence for a few minutes. I sighed. Peg wouldn't be discovering more.

"Maybe I should poke around a bit?"

Brad shook his head. "Do you ever relax?"

~ * ~

While we ate lunch, we whale-watched from the deck of the Pacific Rim restaurant. Duke lapped water from a bowl. "So, where is this compound?" My curiosity was piqued.

"About fifteen minutes from here."

I leaned forward and asked, "Can we drive by and check it out?"

He laughed, "You're like a dog with a bone."

"I can't help it. I'm curious."

"Why not?" We have time. Afterward, we'll drop Duke off at the house. I want to show you Tor House. I signed us up for the one o'clock guided tour if that's OK." He paused. "And then, we'll cruise the seventeen-mile drive."

"Sounds great," I grinned. "What's Tor House?"

"It's the home of a famous California poet, Robinson Jeffers." Brad's eyes twinkled.

Smiling, I placed my hand over my heart. "You're a romantic," I teased.

He put a finger in front of his lips. "Don't tell anyone."

"My lips are sealed." I took a gulp of iced tea as my nerves tingled.

After lunch, we drove the perimeter of Mission Apollo. "Welcome to Mission Apollo" was posted on a large sign next to the front gate. A security guard manned the entrance. Barbed wire topped the concrete fence surrounding the property. Two other gated entrances were likely used for deliveries. It was hard to get a glimpse of anything inside the compound. "Jeez, looks more like a prison," I commented.

"Yeah." Brad tapped his fingers on the steering wheel. "Why all the security? Seems strange."

I silently agreed.

"Want to find out if we can snag a closer look?" he asked.

"Do we have time?" I longed for a deeper view into Apollo's world.

"We should be fine."

I clapped. "Let's do it." I was excited that he'd agreed to indulge my inquiring mind. My mind spun while I concocted a story to justify the visit. "Why don't we say we realized who he was after he left, and we wanted to apologize? We didn't mean to be rude." Duke yipped from the back seat.

"Sounds plausible." Brad drove up to the security gate and explained the situation. The tall, broad-shouldered man looked like he could have been a bouncer in a bar. The guard made a phone call and then leaned out the gatehouse window. "I'm sorry since you have the dog with you, we can't let you on the property. Apollo said you're welcome to come back another time." He handed Brad a clipboard. "If you fill out this form with your contact information, I'll give you a visitor pass. That will save you time when you return."

Brad looked at me. I shrugged, "Why not?"

He filled out the form and handed the clipboard to me. I wrote in my name, address, and driver's license number and passed the documents back to Brad. He exchanged the clipboard for a visitor's pass, made a U-turn, and headed for the house. "I don't think we'll make it back today. How about sometime this week?"

"Sounds good." Although my curiosity was piqued, celebrating Peg's birthday and enjoying Brad's romantic side were higher on my priority list. We dropped Duke off, traded the Rover for Brad's convertible, and drove toward the poet's home. "California Dreamin'" by The Mamas and The Papas streamed from the radio. I released my hair from the pony tail holder and tilted my head toward the sky. The knots in my neck began to melt. As I brought my gaze back to the road, I admired the varying architecture of the houses. I noticed that they were named. "Why do all the homes have names?"

"No street addresses. People identify them by their given name."

The radio switched to a Beach Boy's tune. "I don't see any mailboxes. How do residents get their mail?"

"Post office." He explained. "My assistant lives a few blocks away in Bluebird House. That's how I know."

We arrived at Tor House, and I scanned the pristine grounds while we waited for the other tour participants to join us. I inhaled the scent of nearby pink and yellow roses. Zooming in with my camera lens, I began to snap pictures. Honeybees sipping nectar from sweet asylum. Snap. A California scrub jay perched on the granite stone border. Snap. Sunlight pouring through a window of Hawk Tower. Snap. I released the camera and let it dangle from the strap around my neck. I grinned as I watched hummingbirds dart from flower to flower. Standing on tiptoe, I leaned into Brad and placed a kiss on his cheek. "This is perfect."

As the docent explained the history of Tor House, I studied the structure. The grit and determination of the poet as he'd built the home rock-by-rock resonated in a place deep inside of me. I'd employed a similar determination investigating Peg's death. The artifacts tucked in between stones were fascinating. A shell discovered along the beach. A medallion gifted by a friend. The love story of Robinson and his wife, Una, warmed the chill from the Pacific Ocean. As the tour progressed to the gravesite of the couple's beloved pets, the docent recited a poem inspired by one of Robinson's dogs, and tears poured from my eyes. Brad squeezed my hand.

While I climbed the staircase of Hawk Tower, I reflected on our courtship over the last few months and the current fairy tale moment. The narrow passageway curved and opened into a space at the top of the tower. I banged my knee against one of the boulders as I exited. A cool breeze blew. I shivered, and a sense of unease overcame me. Peg had connived to connect Brad and me, but my relationship history was tainted. Would I ever be able to trust another man again?

After we completed the tour, we continued along the scenic seventeen-mile drive, stopping at key photo ops along the way.

The image of the Lone Cypress surviving amongst a clump of boulders was haunting. After Peg's death and my arrest, I felt like a lone survivor. I recalled the earlier stories about the poet and his wife. What would it be like to have someone by your side like Robinson had with Una?

Chapter 4

Apollo massaged the back of his neck. Troubled by the interruption from the couple and their dog, he replayed his visit to the sacred ground. The holy cavern made the perfect graveyard for the recently departed, and he needed to protect it at all costs. Running into those people had been most unfortunate. The nerve of that pooch growling at him. As he contemplated their brief interaction, he replayed the conversation and his responses. Confident he'd covered his tracks, he breathed a sigh of relief.

He reflected on how he'd overcome his upbringing. Could you even call it homeschooled when you didn't have a home? When his parents passed, he was eighteen and had barely learned to read and write. It'd taken him two years to earn his GED and another eight to obtain his degree from California State University in Monterey Bay. His psychology major and business minor came in handy in the day-to-day management of the compound. After everything he'd invested, he wasn't about to let anyone ruin it all. His thoughts were interrupted by a call from the guard at the gate.

That woman was trouble. His mind churned as he strode toward the entrance to pick up the forms with the additional information on the pair. Armed with names, addresses, and driver's license numbers, he couldn't wait to conduct a search on the meddlers.

He stared at his computer as he read the news stories about Liz Adams and her friend Peg's death. The image of her friend was familiar. He'd seen her once on the sacred grounds a few years ago. Apollo was surprised to discover Peg had been a kindred spirit in the mission to help the homeless. Even if Liz had been cleared of any foul play, he wasn't confident she didn't have some part in poor Peg's death. After all, it was her gun, and the local police sure didn't have anything positive to say about her. He shook his head as he drummed his fingers on the table. That woman tainted the sacred ground. She needed to return to South Carolina. Fast.

He switched his attention to Brad O'Connor. Some big-shot CEO of an identity theft protection company. Apollo recognized the company's name. The guy was filthy rich. Maybe he could hit him up for a donation. A sinister grin spread across his face. Apollo could sell their identities. Now wouldn't that be an interesting twist?

He tucked the idea aside, summoned one of his Disciples, and tasked him with the job of researching the couple's backgrounds. Then he placed a call to the number on the form for Liz. He was pleased when she answered on the second ring and agreed to a tour the facility tomorrow at two. He'd make it a visit to remember.

Chapter 5

Since I had some time before our planned dinner to celebrate Peg's birthday, I fired up my computer and ran a search on Mission Apollo. I found several articles that praised the Mission's efforts to help the homeless. As I dug deeper, I discovered some chat groups that speculated about possible drugs on the compound, as well as a family member who claimed that after the Mission picked her brother up, he went missing.

Fifteen minutes later, I slipped on a long-sleeved lavender dress with a flared hem, added a pair of black flats, and quickly touched up my make-up. I wanted to wear heels, but I knew we'd be wandering around the town shopping and taking in the sights. As I fluffed my wind-tossed hair out with dry shampoo, I hoped Peg would approve of my outfit. Her favorite color was purple. Spritzing on a fresh layer of Amazing Grace, I emerged from the guest bedroom and bumped into Brad.

"Don't you look nice." He pulled me close, placed a soft kiss on my mouth, and then nuzzled my neck. "You're wearing my favorite scent," he whispered.

Oh my! Would I make it through tonight without giving my bruised heart away? The butterflies had already started fluttering, and I felt vulnerable after the day's events. I missed Peg like crazy, and I hadn't yet adjusted to the time change. Honestly, how well did I know this man? Sure, he looked dashing, dressed in a lavender shirt with a navy sports coat and gray pants, but how could I be sure he wasn't exactly like my ex, Sawyer? He'd seemed charming in the beginning as well.

I stepped back and smoothed my dress. "I hope Duke doesn't mind that we're not taking him with us." I worried about leaving him alone in a new place.

"He'll be fine. I think he's kind of getting used to his new digs," Brad grinned. "And we won't be gone long. We need to make it a bit of an early night since we have the meeting with Tim in the morning."

We started our celebration by strolling the grounds of the Carmel Mission. The late afternoon sun lessened the effect of the chill in the air. As we toured the gardens, a hummingbird hovered between the two of us. I grabbed Brad's arm. "Peg asked me to think of her whenever I saw a hummingbird."

"It's a sign." He sighed. "Happy Birthday, Peg."

I snapped a picture with my phone of the nearby outdoor fountain surrounded by pink, yellow, and purple flowers and messaged it to my mom and dad in Florida. *Enjoying Carmel, love you guys.* Since I was an only child, if I didn't call or text every couple of days, they worried.

When we entered the Mission's cemetery, the same earlier sense of unease overcame me. The wooden cross and abalone shell marked gravesites of the Native Americans were eerie. I shivered.

"You cold?" Brad slipped off his jacket and placed it around my shoulders.

"Thanks." Was my mind trying to ruin a perfectly lovely day, or was my gut trying to tell me something?

After the Mission, Brad drove by a few of the famous fairy tale cottages. While I rolled down the window, I listened as Brad described how Hugh Comstock lovingly designed the home named Hansel for his wife, Mayotta. Carmel seemed to be filled with love stories. I snapped a few more pictures and sent them to my parents.

He parked the car in downtown Carmel, and we strolled hand-in-hand along the sidewalk. Brad commented, "It's a good thing you didn't wear heels."

I glanced down at my shoes and laughed. "Yeah, the pavement's a little uneven."

"It's not only that. You could actually get a ticket for wearing them."

"Get out." I tugged at Brad's sleeve.

He held up three fingers. "Scout's honor. It's a city ordinance. You need a permit for any heel over two inches."

A serious revolt would occur if they ever tried to pass a law like that in Charleston.

"Why don't you explore the shops while I check our reservation?"

"Excuse to escape shopping?" I teased.

Brad gave me a sheepish grin. "Yeah."

We agreed to meet at the restaurant for cocktails at six. As I wandered in and out of the art galleries and shops, I slowly accumulated purchases for my neighbors and myself. I even snagged a few new toys for Duke at the local pet shop.

Arms full of bags, I entered Anton's fifteen minutes late. I was surprised to find Brad at the end of the bar with another woman.

He stood and greeted me with a kiss. Motioning to the bar stool next to him, he introduced me to his companion. "Liz, this is Sam.

I was filling her in on our encounter with Apollo. She's with the Carmel police force."

Jeez, not another cop named Sam. Seriously? The last one was a male, and he'd arrested me as a suspect in Peg's murder. I liked the female version of Sam better. With brunette hair that hit her shoulder blades and a flawless olive complexion, her appearance was much easier on the eyes than the other Sam. She was in better shape than I was. Although I'd been told by a mutual friend that Brad preferred blondes, I wondered about the history between the two of them.

"Nice to meet you, Liz. I'm waiting on a to-go order, and then I'll be out of your hair." Dang, even her voice was sexy. "No telling when someone will call about another lost wallet or cell phone," she joked.

"So, there's not a lot of crime here?" I inquired.

"Very little. The occasional alleged theft, which usually winds up being a lost item that's later returned." She laughed.

A few moments later, Sam's food arrived, and she left. By the knowing looks between the two of them, I sensed Brad's relationship with her was more complicated than he let on, but I let my curiosity go. Tonight was about celebrating Peg.

The bartender handed me a glass of merlot as the hostess tapped Brad on the shoulder. "Sir, your table is ready."

She ushered us to a table for two by the window in the corner. An arrangement of cream-colored roses was perfectly centered on a peach linen tablecloth. The glass vase reflected the surrounding tea lights.

Brad pulled the chair out for me and then took his seat.

"This was one of Peg's favorite places?" I asked as I perused the menu.

"Yup. She loved the free-range chicken. The rack of lamb is my favorite, and the iceberg wedge salad is really good."

Our server arrived, and we placed our orders. Brad raised his glass. "Happy Birthday, Peg."

"To Peg." As our glasses clinked, my eyes misted with tears. Brad cleared his throat, excused himself, and headed toward the men's room. Today marked what would have been her thirty-seventh birthday. Earlier, Brad had called her brother, Ian. I could tell by his pained look during the conversation that the call had been a tough one. Life was so unfair. I said a silent prayer for her family. My phone pinged with a message from Lou, Peg's former business partner, and friend.

> Thinking about you. Missing Peg like crazy. How are things with Brad?

> Me too. :(All good with Brad.

I added the symbol for hugs and hit 'send.' Seconds later, I had a group text from my other neighbors, Linda, Gwen, Cassie, and Maria, as each of them remembered Peg's birthday. The absence of her presence was a huge void in our lives.

Brad returned with red-rimmed eyes as the server arrived with our wedge salads. I sliced into the iceberg lettuce, took a bite, and sighed with contentment. Topped with Gorgonzola instead of blue cheese, the flavors of the peppered bacon and artichoke dressing complemented each other. I steered the conversation to a subject that wouldn't cause either of us to break down in tears. "I did some Googling when we got back to the house. Apollo is an interesting character."

"What'd you find?"

"The usual feel-good articles about his mission of saving the homeless. Then some odd chat groups speculating that all is not as it appears."

"Like what?"

"Rumors of drug use and people gone missing."

"Hmm." He rubbed his chin. "I asked Sam about Apollo. She said the compound is pretty quiet. The police rarely get called out there. The last time it happened, Apollo claimed it was a false alarm."

"So. What's the deal with you and Sam?" Ugh, I'd so promised myself I would not go there. "Sorry. Never mind. It's none of my business."

Brad's eyes twinkled. "Jealous?"

"Well, she is drop-dead gorgeous."

He set his fork down and grabbed both of my hands. "Liz, you have no idea how beautiful you are, do you?" While he gazed into my eyes, he continued, "Trust me. You don't have to worry about Sam."

After my experience with my ex, I wasn't taking anything at face value. Sawyer used to say I was beautiful, too, even while he cheated on me.

The waiter arrived and cleared away our salads. I was grateful for the interruption. Brad ordered a bottle of wine to go with our entrees.

When the server departed, he asked, "What made you decide to become a private investigator?"

I filled Brad in on my divorce from my ex, and my journey to Charleston to pursue a dream of being involved in law enforcement. Then our entrees arrived, and the server poured a splash of pinot noir into Brad's glass. After he swirled the ruby liquid, he took a sip. "Perfect." Brad dismissed the waiter, filled our glasses, and then responded to my answer. "That had to be a tough change. New place, new career."

"Meeting Peg was a godsend. She helped me settle in and get acclimated to the area." I paused to take a bite of the chicken that was so tender I didn't need a knife. "Between the sale of my house in Atlanta and some stock options from my corporate job, I was able to survive financially." I sighed and tasted another forkful of the meat. "I was lucky to work with BridgePoint Investigations. The owner, Gunner, is a very well-respected PI in the Charleston community. Of course, Peg's connections helped when I went solo."

"Do you have a specialty?"

"Jack of all trades," I responded.

Scratching the back of his head, he asked, "How does that work?"

"Believe me, there's plenty of PI work to go around between cheating spouses, insurance scams—"

"And murders," he interrupted.

"Yeah." I sighed. "Those too."

~ * ~

After dinner, we returned to the house, where I unloaded my packages and gave Duke his new toys. His tail thumped against the wall while he debated which one to pick up first. He settled on the soft bunny and turned circles as the toy squeaked. "I think he likes them." I ruffled the fur on his back. "Good boy."

"How about I fire up the hot tub, and we have one more glass of wine?" Brad asked.

"Sounds good." My muscles ached from this morning's trek. I was pleasantly full from the evening's meal. Relaxing in the hot tub would be a perfect end to the night. I hurried to change into my swimsuit and joined Brad outside.

As I settled into the water, I leaned my head back, admired the stars, and allowed the jets to work their magic. The sky was perfectly clear, and a sliver of a moon hung overhead. P!nk's "Glitter in the Air" drifted through the outdoor speakers. Brad handed me a plastic wine glass and slipped his arm around my shoulder. Exhausted from the day's events, Duke was curled up on the deck with his bunny. I placed my toes against the pulsating jets and let the push of the water ease my aching feet.

"What do you think of Carmel so far?"

"It's great," I replied. "We packed a lot of sightseeing into today."

"Was it too much? I wanted you to experience a decent taste of Carmel since I have to work tomorrow."

"It was perfect." I nuzzled in closer. He'd let me know before I arrived that he'd be working all day Monday and most mornings while I was in town. He was taking Tuesday, Wednesday, and Thursday afternoons off. My original plan had been to lounge by the pool while he was gone. Guess tomorrow's plans had changed.

"We're lucky to have such a clear night," Brad commented. "July's typically foggy."

I leaned my head back on his arm and sighed. "Do you think Peg's up there watching us?"

"Of course, she's in heaven. But I hope she's not watching." He kissed my neck and made his way to my lips. I set my glass down and melted into his embrace.

Chapter 6

Apollo watched the children play on the school's playground. At least his parents had taken him to parks so that he'd some interaction with other children. He remembered how lonely it'd been on the property and how he'd discovered and explored the cavern. When he got older, his mom had taken him to woodshop and gardening classes. Sports were forbidden. He'd never considered how she paid for the lessons.

He shook his head and continued on. As he contemplated Liz's upcoming visit, Apollo brainstormed the possibilities. Perhaps he could convince the woman to donate the land to his cause. Or better yet, convince the boyfriend, Brad, to donate a couple million. After all their friend had been determined to help the homeless. He stopped by the kitchen and requested a special batch of cookies for tomorrow's tour. On his way back to the main building, he bumped into a Newbie.

"Sorry, sir." The pint-sized man stepped out of his way.

Apollo looked at the man's name tag, 'Peanut.' Putting on

his best fake smile, Apollo said, "Quite alright, just watch where you're going." Fool, he thought as he patted the small man's arm. What kind of name was Peanut?

Back in his office, Apollo called and arranged for the Disciples to give short presentations at various places where he'd take Liz. Of course, the tour would skip the underground drug warehouse. Then he prepped and rehearsed a convincing speech. As he pushed his hair off his forehead, he smiled. He'd turn up the charm. There'd be no way she could refuse his request.

~ * ~

Peanut shuddered and brushed off the spot where Apollo had touched him. He needed to be more careful. The last thing he wanted to do was draw attention to himself. He'd just filled out his application and interviewed for the job in the garden. Saying a silent prayer that he'd get the gig, he scurried on. He couldn't get out of there soon enough, and exploring the outdoors would provide him with the best options for escape.

Chapter 7

I awoke to the smell of sweat and coffee. Duke was curled at the end of the bed. His tail thumped when Brad entered the room after his workout. Gratefully accepting the mug he offered, I blushed.

While Brad stroked Duke's back, he averted my gaze. "Are you OK?" He hastily added, "I mean about last night . . . I hope I didn't go there too fast."

My face was officially on fire. "Hey, I was a willing participant. I'm fine. It was good." I took a big sip of coffee and clutched the mug as memories of the night rushed forth. We'd had a little too much wine, and the evening had progressed from the hot tub to his bedroom. But it *was* good, *really good*.

He raised his head and studied my eyes.

After a sip of coffee, I changed the subject. "What time do we leave for the office?"

"In about an hour. Our meeting with Tim is at nine." He paused and then kissed my cheek. "I'm so glad you're here."

"Me, too." I smiled.

"I'll take a shower and then I'll make us a big breakfast." Duke's tail thumped again at the word "breakfast."

As I sat in his bed and sipped my coffee, I watched the waves roll into shore through the open blinds. I had to admit the previous evening had been amazing. More than that. It was joyful...like nothing I'd ever experienced before. Yet, everything was happening so fast, and I felt unsure of myself. Damn Peg for conniving to put us together from the other side. I bet she was laughing her ass off at my dilemma.

Brad hummed some tune in the shower. I climbed out of bed, slipped a slightly damp cover-up over my head, and snatched my bathing suit off the wooden floor. "C'mon Duke." I headed for the guest bathroom. I needed a bit of space.

~ * ~

While Brad drove toward MultiPoint Protection's offices, we sat in awkward silence and listened to this morning's news stream through the radio. Even though the office was pet friendly, we'd decided to leave Duke at his place.

I fished in my purse for my favorite lipstick, then lowered the mirror on the visor and applied a fresh coat of coral. "How much longer?" I asked.

"About another ten minutes."

"What can I expect when we arrive?" Comfortable talking shop, I put last night's events out of my mind. *For the moment.*

He turned down the radio and briefed me on the meeting with his CFO. "Tim pulled the details from the four cases we've had to date. He'll fill you in at a high level, and then if you want you can review the data in detail." He reached over and rubbed my leg. "I appreciate you doing this."

The nerve endings in my thigh hummed at his touch. While I gazed out the window at the passing scenery, images of the previous evening replayed in my mind. I glanced back at Brad. His eyes were glued to the road, and his hands tightly gripped the wheel. My gaze settled on his lips, and my stomach quivered. I tore my eyes away and mentally shifted back to the business at hand. I knew how important this was to him, and I had to admit my curiosity was piqued. I hoped I could help him.

~ * ~

We entered the building, and I admired the slate blue walls that met floor-to-ceiling windows. Brown leather couches and chairs were arranged around glass-topped tables. The receptionist's desk was wood with a stainless-steel top. Polished plank wood floors shone a rich umber and reflected light from crystal chandeliers hanging overhead. "Peg's work?"

"Yeah. I fought her on the chandeliers. I wanted more of a high-tech vibe. Peg was right. The space needed a homey touch. Something that says you can trust us with your data."

Brad made small talk with the receptionist as I signed the guest log. He pulled a biscuit out of his pocket and gave it to the Maltipoo curled in a dog bed next to her chair.

As I clipped the visitor's badge to my jacket, we headed down the hallway. "How many employees do you have?"

"A hundred and three and growing."

"All full-time?" I asked.

"We have a few part-timers. No contractors. You either work for us or you don't."

A thin woman in her sixties guarded the entrance to his spacious office. Her gray hair was pulled back in a tight bun, and she wore a stern look on her face. There was no pet in her workspace.

"Alice, this is Liz. She's a friend of mine."

Alice nodded as I shook her bony hand. I wasn't sure how I felt about the friend comment. After last night was that all we were? Friends with benefits? At least I didn't have to worry about a hot administrative assistant.

"Alice is my right arm," Brad continued. "Keeps me straight. I don't know what I'd do without her."

Her pursed lips turned up in a half-smile. "Pleased to meet you, Liz. Can I bring you anything to drink?"

"A glass of water would be great."

Brad cleared some folders off an ebony rectangular conference table for six. Two crystal chandeliers hung overhead. "Have a seat." He shut the blinds on the windows behind us.

I sat in one of the ergonomically correct chairs and checked out the room. Anchoring the other end of the space was a massive black u-shaped desk and bookshelves with a collection of business books. On top of the desk were three computer monitors. The only relief in the sea of black and white was the Blue Dog artwork and the strategically placed fresh greenery. Crystal accents reflected the overhead lights.

Alice returned, followed by a man whom I assumed was Tim. He was under six feet and had a receding hairline. Glasses perched on his nose, outlining kind, topaz eyes. I took an immediate liking to him. Alice set our drinks down then exited, and we got down to business.

Brad introduced us and then filled Tim in on my background. He added that I was here to assess the situation and hopefully refer them to someone who would take on the case. Turning his attention to me, he said, "We discovered the thefts thanks to Tim. We're developing some new software that searches for duplicate identification numbers issued in different names. It's all hush-hush as the U.S. government is interested in using the program to detect voter fraud. One of Tim's friends who recently passed away popped up as a victim. A synthetic identity was used to open a bank account. It was also used to fill several different online prescription orders. Tim's kept a close watch on our data ever since."

I knew just enough about synthetic identity theft to know that was when real information and fake information were combined to create a new identity. The victim wasn't out any money, but eventually, something goes awry.

Tim commented, "The new software will find it early on once we get the bugs worked out."

"We're way ahead of our competition," Brad added.

Tim passed a set of folders over to me. "In each one are the details of the four cases to date. The first folder is my friend's case. All of the victims are deceased." He gave a high-level summary of each theft as I thumbed through the file.

"Have you notified the authorities?"

"There's a copy of the police report in each file. Identity theft isn't high on their priority list."

Brad added, "Especially when the victim is deceased."

"We're hoping this isn't the beginning of a bigger effort. All of our clients could be at risk."

Brad interjected, "It's all the more reason we'd like this solved sooner rather than later."

"Are there any patterns?" I asked.

"Other than the victims being deceased, the addresses for the new identities are scattered across San Jose. In every case, new bank accounts were opened, and online prescription orders were filled."

I leaned forward and asked, "Who knows about the new software?"

"Like I said, it's all hush-hush. Just myself, Tim, and a couple of software engineers."

"How do you store each individual's information?"

"We have digital files that are regularly backed up. Early on, we also had paper files," Tim answered.

"Trust me. Everything is very secure. That's what makes this so unbelievable," Brad added.

"How do you know when someone has passed?"

Tim responded, "Usually a family member calls in and cancels the service. Then we mark the file as deceased."

As the questions flowed from my lips, I jotted down notes. "Any employee recently make any major purchases? Or go on big trips?"

"We pay our employees well. They're constantly taking trips and buying stuff." Brad rubbed the back of his neck. "I'll think about it. I'd hate it if this was an inside job."

"Have you reviewed your computer records to see who's accessed the files?"

"Of course," Tim replied. "That was one of the first things we did. Nothing was out of the ordinary. The details are in the folders."

I pressed on. "Any disgruntled ex-employees?"

"Our turnover is pretty low." Brad paused and rubbed his chin. "There was the guy in customer service who left at the beginning of the year. What was his name?"

"Mitch. He was with us for a year. Customer service wasn't his thing. Got a job as an analyst with one of our competitors, SecureLife."

"Anita left last month once her maternity leave ran out. Decided to stay home with her baby girl. Can't blame her, she's a doll." Brad smiled. "She was one of our first software engineers. There's no way she had anything to do with this."

I noted both names.

"Maybe it will help if you see the organization." Tim pulled a chart out of another folder and passed it my way. "We don't have a lot of layers. Underneath the four VPs are team leads. The teams tend to flex. So the reporting lines aren't always clear." He leaned over and pointed to three boxes on the chart. "Those are the engineers working with me on the development of the new product."

"What other information do you need, Liz?" Brad asked.

As I licked my lips, I had to admit I was intrigued. I'd investigated plenty of insurance scams. This would be my first identity theft case. I could pull in experts. Yes, I was supposed to be on vacation, but the challenge was enticing.

Brad massaged his forehead with his fingertips. "Do you know someone who can solve this mess?"

"Before I answer, I do have a few more questions." My pulse quickened. "Do you have a time frame in mind?"

"I'd like to wrap this up in two weeks."

I licked my lips and continued, "How much access will the investigator have to records and the employees?"

Brad responded, "As much as they need. This is important to me."

"Hmm, it's not my area of expertise, but I can bring in help as needed…" I locked eyes with Brad. "What do you think about me taking the lead on the investigation?"

"You're supposed to be taking a break."

"I can do that later. I know how much this means to you."

Brad hesitated. "Tim?"

"Up to you, boss," he replied.

Grinning dimple to dimple, Brad stood and placed a hand on my shoulder. "It's a huge relief knowing you're on the case."

"When can I start?"

Brad responded. "As soon as you'd like. We can set you up in Tim's office with a company laptop so you can access the personnel files."

I shrugged. "Well then, Tim, show me the way." As I looked back over my shoulder at Brad, I said, "I'll send you a proposal. You're not getting off cheap." I winked.

~ * ~

Tim walked me to his office down the hall. "You can use the conference table. I'll call IT and get them to bring you a laptop."

"Thanks."

He introduced me to his cat. "This is Irish. I hope you don't mind cats."

"Not at all." I bent down to pet the plump black feline.

"I'm going to grab another cup of coffee. You need anything?"

"No, thanks. While I wait for IT, I'll work off my laptop. What's the password for the Wi-Fi?"

After I signed in with a jumble of letters, symbols, and numbers, I drafted a proposal with fees and emailed it to Brad and Tim. I got an immediate reply from Brad—Accepted. Irish wound in and out of my legs. I wondered how he and Duke would get along.

Not long after Tim returned, an employee from IT arrived with the computer and gave me a short lesson on how to use the programs. That was fast. I pulled my index cards out of my tote, logged into the company's HR system, and started creating a card for each employee with pertinent information such as age, marital status, and work history. I'd add physical characteristics and social history later. Tim and I worked alongside each other in comfortable silence. I was about halfway through when Alice entered and interrupted us both.

"Lunch is ready." She placed a boxed meal on Tim's desk and motioned for me to follow her. "Brad would like for you to join him in his office."

I turned toward Tim. "You're not coming?"

"Nah, I usually work through lunch."

"Turkey or chicken?" Brad asked as I took the seat next to him.

"I'll take the chicken."

"We provide lunch for all our employees. Takes too long to drive to a restaurant and back. I asked Alice to grab a couple of boxes for us. She'll add you to the email distribution so you'll know when lunch has arrived."

"OK." I took a sip from the glass of iced tea set on the coaster next to my meal. "I've been reviewing the files, and I'd like to interview some of your employees. What do you think about introducing me as a consultant who's reviewing your processes and identifying areas for improvement?"

"Good idea. You might want to use a different name. If anyone Googled you..." he trailed off.

"You're right." Being a suspect in Peg's death had put me in the headlines. Although Liz Adams was a common name, my picture appeared as well. "How about Liz Butler? Butler was my maiden name."

"Works for me."

I wondered how long the investigation would take. Originally, I'd planned to fly out on Friday, right after Brad's birthday. I hadn't brought enough clothes for an extended stay.

As if he'd read my mind, he continued, "I'd really like this mess settled in a couple of weeks. Our employees and clients depend upon us. If word ever got out . . ." His shoulders slumped. "I hate to even think about it . . . I know you didn't plan to stay that long. You can still take the plane back on Friday, pick up whatever you need, and then return on Sunday." He added, "By the way, feel free to use one of my cars while you're here."

"What about Duke?"

"He can stay with me." He reached over and patted my thigh. "Don't worry. I'll take good care of him."

"OK." I took a bite of my chicken salad sandwich. "This is delicious."

"Comes from a local deli. It's usually my first choice."

"Oh. Sorry, I took your favorite." I actually wasn't sorry. The chicken mixture with cashews, red onion, and spinach on a whole-wheat bun was tasty.

"No worries. I like the turkey too." He swallowed a bite of his sandwich. "So? What are your initial thoughts?"

If he bugged me constantly about the case, I'd go crazy. I needed to establish some ground rules. "It's too soon for that. Right now, I'm gathering facts." When I'd worked for Bridgepoint, I'd learned from my mentor, Gunner, not to jump to early conclusions. "How about I give you a status report at the end of the week? Either written or verbal. Whichever you prefer."

Brad squinted. "I need more than that. How about a verbal debrief at the end of each day?"

"That works."

While I'd perused the police reports, I'd wondered if Sam was involved in the investigation, but I hadn't come across her name. Before I took another bite of chicken salad, I asked, "Is Sam investigating the thefts?"

"I told her about it. But it's out of her jurisdiction. She doesn't want to step on any toes."

We ate in silence for a few minutes. "Um, about us." I tore open the bag of barbecue chips.

"What about us?"

Averting my gaze from his eyes to the chips, I lowered my voice. "Maybe it's not such a good idea for us to be romantically involved while this is going on . . . or at least not be affectionate in the office or in public."

"Yeah, probably a good idea," he conceded.

Might as well get this over now. I didn't think I would have the same resolve back at the house. "I also think it's better if we sleep in separate rooms for now. I'll feel more comfortable."

Brad frowned. "What do you mean?"

My face grew warm. "We can still . . . you know." I shrugged. "But I'd prefer to sleep in my own bed."

After a moment he said, "OK. If that's what you want."

I half-wished he'd put up a bigger protest. We finished the rest of our meals in uncomfortable silence.

Chapter 8

A woman with the number three tattooed on her right wrist greeted me at the door when I arrived at the main building on the compound at two p.m. sharp. Brad had a business meeting and couldn't join me. As she ushered me into the lobby, I surveyed the surroundings. A pair of orange couches lined one wall. Black and white photos of the compound hung above the worn seats. The security guard perched behind a pine desk nodded at me. Within minutes, Apollo entered. His presence filled the space. "Greetings, Liz. Welcome to Mission Apollo." His strained smile didn't match his words.

"Thank you for inviting me. I admire your efforts to help the homeless. My friend, Peg, would've, too. It was a cause she felt strongly about."

"Ah, yes. Ms. Peg Kelley-Thomas of Charleston. I was saddened to learn of her passing." He adjusted the collar of his starched shirt. "She and I were kindred spirits."

"How did you know Peg?" I asked.

"I met her once on the property where I met you," he explained. "I assume she left the land to you?"

I nodded. Surely Peg would have mentioned meeting Apollo to me. Something didn't ring true. I wished that I had Duke with me.

"I'm anxious to show you the facility and all the good we do here." He added, "I think your friend, Peg, would've approved." He held open the door. "Shall we begin?"

As we walked, Apollo related the tale of his life-journey. The sing-song sound of his voice was pleasant and alluring. "My parents were from a wealthy family but were free spirits. They believed in living off the land. I grew up in a tent not far from here." He paused for effect. "The cold nights and thunderstorms were torturous." He shook his head. "Everyone deserves a roof over their heads." After he ushered me to the first stop, the barracks, he turned the conversation over to a Disciple who described the living quarters. Apollo studied my face as I scanned the space.

Rows of perfectly made bunk beds lined the walls. A separate room contained lockers where the inhabitants could store their belongings. At the opposite end of the structure was a bathroom with communal showers. The room we were in was for women and children. The men occupied a separate building. Apollo must have noticed my frown, and he quickly explained, "We discourage procreation. Our space is limited, and we wish to accommodate everyone we can. We're currently working on plans for additional buildings."

As we headed for the chapel, Apollo picked up his story, "I had no idea my parents were wealthy until they passed. With the money they left me, I began to develop the compound." When we arrived at the on-site school, he stopped. "Class is in session, so we won't interrupt." He thrust his chin forward as he spoke. "Our children receive an excellent education, and our student-to-teacher ratio is very good. If you'd like to come back another time, I can arrange for you to meet our teachers." He extended his arm and motioned for me to move on. "Faith is an important part of our program. The chapel is where we worship."

"Why do some of the women have number tattoos?" I asked.

"They have special jobs within the Mission. It helps us to identify them," he replied before turning the tour over to the Disciple stationed in the chapel. Apollo stood by his side and listened as the Disciple began his presentation.

Puzzled by Apollo's comment, I yearned to ask more questions. As the Disciple droned on, I observed the worship space. Immediately I noticed there was only one small entrance. Maybe there was another door in the back. There were no windows. Instead, stained-glass skylights in the ceiling cast a rainbow of colors on handcrafted wooden pews. A marble altar loomed in front. A golden tapestry hung behind it. The hairs on my arm rose. I involuntarily shivered.

Interrupting the presentation, I turned to Apollo and asked, "Why are some people called Disciples?"

He thrust his chest forward. "Ah. They are the Chosen Ones, called to critical positions within the Mission."

He must've caught the quizzical look on my face because he cleared his throat and added, "It's important to have some sort of structure. After years on the streets, our Members need predictability."

We strode toward the cafeteria and, Apollo expounded on the Mission and the various jobs the Members performed on the compound.

As he held the door of the dining hall open for me, he asked, "What will you do with all that land?"

"I haven't decided."

"I've been thinking about expanding. Would you consider donating it to the Mission?" He placed his hand on my arm and added, "Wouldn't it be a wonderful way to honor your friend? Helping the homeless. Something that meant so much to her."

I took a step back. "I'd like to learn more before making such a big decision."

He dropped his hand. "Of course, let's continue." As the next Disciple explained the various jobs in the kitchen, my eyes scanned the room. Long tables lined the main area. A cafeteria-style buffet space flanked the far wall. In a corner of the room, a woman mopped the floors. The place was pristine. Apollo picked up a tray of cookies and offered one to me. Not wanting to be impolite, I picked up a chocolate chip cookie and took a bite. "Delicious. Thank you."

"It's our own special recipe." Apollo winked at his Disciple. "Would you like something to drink? Perhaps some milk?"

"A glass of water would be great, thank you."

The Disciple filled a Styrofoam cup with ice and water and handed it to me. We continued on our tour to the last stops, the gardens and the sick bay.

"Why so much security?" I asked. I'd spotted guards stationed at various locations around the compound.

Apollo cleared his throat. "We've had some outsiders who don't believe in what we do try to disrupt our operations." He brushed his hair off his shoulders then added, "And we like to protect the privacy of our Members."

Once we arrived back at the main building, Apollo asked, "So? What do you think?"

"You are doing incredible work here at the Mission. I wish Peg had a chance to see this place."

Apollo's brows raised, and he leaned in closer with a hopeful smile.

I hastily added, "I just don't think it's the right choice to donate the land."

His face fell. "Well then, thank you for stopping by."

"If I change my mind, I'll let you know. Thank you for the tour."

Apollo turned his back to me and walked to his office without responding.

Chapter 9

As I climbed into Brad's car, I felt dizzy and a little nauseous. I cranked up the air conditioner and pointed the vents toward my face before turning onto the street. About a mile down the road, I had to pull to the side. My vision had blurred, and I didn't want to wreck Brad's car. I placed a call to him, explained the situation, and gave him my location.

"Do you need medical help?"

"I'm fine. Just a little woozy, and I don't feel comfortable driving. It feels like I've had a few drinks too many."

"I'll be right there. I'll get Tim to drop me off."

Brad rapped on the driver's side window. I jerked upright. I'd fallen into a deep sleep. After unlocking the door, I pulled myself out of the car. My knees were wobbly. Brad grabbed my arm.

"Are you OK?" Concern clouded his face. He walked me to the passenger side of his vehicle.

"I will be."

After he'd buckled himself into the driver's seat, he commented. "Your eyes are red. What happened?"

I described my tour of Mission Apollo. "There might have been something in those cookies. Apollo said it was a special recipe."

"You mean a drug?"

I nodded.

"That's just wrong. Why would he do something like that?" Brad's lips pursed, and he gripped the steering wheel as he pulled back out onto the road.

I shook my head and replied, "I don't know. The whole experience was beyond weird."

~ * ~

Back in my room, tucked safely under the covers with Duke at my feet, my mind spun over the day's events. Brad had introduced me to the employees after lunch. The population was diverse in age, race, and nationality.

My visit to Mission Apollo was bizarre. Although everything appeared pristine, a sinister undercurrent had hummed through the compound. I was pretty certain I'd been drugged. My head still throbbed.

Tomorrow I planned to review the folders and then prioritize the list of employees for interviews around their work processes. Brad had given me a rather chaste kiss goodnight. The hamster wheel in my head whirled around the state of our relationship and what direction it was headed. Duke hopped off the bed and whined at the door.

"Really, boy? I just took you out."

He answered with another whine.

"OK. I'm coming."

As soon as I opened the door, he headed in the opposite direction straight down the hall to Brad's room. He sat in front of his door and barked.

"Duke. No. Hush." I grabbed his collar and attempted to tug him back down the hall.

Brad opened the door. "What's up?" He wore pajama bottoms and no top. I couldn't help but stare at the well-defined muscles in his chest.

"Sorry. I don't know what his problem is. I thought he needed to go out."

Maneuvering out of his collar, Duke jumped onto Brad's bed.

"Looks like he wants to hang with me." He grinned.

"Traitor." I strode toward the bed and slipped his collar back over his neck.

Brad wrapped his arms around me. "Join us? I promise to behave." He tenderly tucked a stray hair behind my ear. "Please, you scared me today."

I took a deep breath and sighed. "OK."

A few hours later, I awoke to the sound of Brad screaming, "Help!" over and over. As he thrashed about in the sheets, I shook his shoulder and tried to wake him up. Duke whined and pawed Brad's legs. Finally, his eyes fluttered open, and he sat upright. He took a long swig from the bottle of water on the nightstand. Sweat poured from his temples. "Jesus, that hasn't happened in a while."

"Are you alright?" I asked. He looked dazed and visibly shaken.

"I will be. Give me a minute," he responded as Duke nudged his way closer. "Hey, buddy." He massaged my dog's ears.

I went to the bathroom, fetched a hand towel, and handed it to him. "What just happened?"

Brad mopped the sweat off his brow. "A nightmare. My sister." He took a few deep breaths. "I have horrible dreams about her drowning accident. It used to happen a lot. The last time was right after Peg's death."

I waited for him to continue.

"I was thirteen when it happened. My friends and I were playing hoops in the driveway when I heard my mom scream. Kristin was such a little fish. She was on the swim team." He shook his head. "No one thought twice about leaving her alone in the pool. We think she hit her head on the side while swimming laps. When Mom found her, it was too late."

I rubbed Brad's arm. "I'm so sorry. I can't imagine how awful that was. Is that why you have the safety cover on the pool?"

"Yeah." He took another long sip from the bottle. "It took me forever to get back in the water. Every swimming part of a triathlon, I dedicate to her. I wear an alert device in case anything happens to me while I'm training." He sighed. "I want you to wear one too if you're in the pool by yourself."

He put his arm around me and pulled me close. "I'm sorry I put you through that. I don't know if the nightmares will ever go away."

"It's OK." I reached for his hand and interlaced his fingers with mine. "No need to apologize."

Duke snatched the damp towel off the bed and shook it. "Give me that." Brad laughed as he attempted to wrestle the cloth from his jaws.

"Drop," I added in a stern tone.

Duke let go, and Brad tossed the towel on the floor. "Let's all try to get some sleep. We have another big day tomorrow."

I'd never had a sibling. I couldn't imagine what it was like to have one and then lose them so tragically. As I cuddled next to Brad, I draped my arm over his body and pulled him close.

~ * ~

While Brad was on his morning bike ride, I placed a call to Gunner. He picked up the phone right away.

"What's up, Liz?"

"I'm in California working on an identity theft case." I didn't remember any identity theft cases that were handled by Gunner's firm while I was there, but I was hoping he might have some later experience to pass on.

"How'd you end up working a case in California?"

"Long story."

"You have a license?"

"No. Good point." I made a mental note to take care of that detail. Although, I wasn't positive I needed a California license, since technically I was posing as a consultant. I continued, "Have you worked on any identity theft cases?"

"Sure. Several."

"Any advice?" I picked up a pen to take notes.

"Follow the money trail. If the thief made a purchase, see if it was made in person. Call the store and ask to look at any video footage. You may want to pull in a computer expert. I have a contact I can forward to you. What type of theft are we talking about?"

I filled him in on the details.

"Tread carefully. Might be connected to a gang or cartel."

"I will." I hesitated. "Um, I need some advice on something else." I doodled on the legal pad in front of me.

"Shoot."

"I broke a golden rule." Sighing, I dropped the pen and slumped in the kitchen chair. "I'm involved with the client." I expanded on the history of our relationship.

"Some rules are made to be broken." I could envision Gunner shrugging on the other end.

As I rubbed the knots in the back of my neck, I asked, "What's that supposed to mean?"

"It means it's not always about work, Liz. You've been through a lot lately. He sounds special. The whole tone of your voice changed while you were talking about him."

I'd never met Gunner's wife. She'd died of cancer before we met. He said she had been the love of his life. They'd been married for twenty-five years.

"Listen, kid. I gotta run. Keep me posted and call me anytime."

Brad walked into the kitchen when I ended the call. He was freshly showered and dressed for work. He smelled like leather and cloves. "Who was on the phone?" he asked as he grabbed a bottle of water from the fridge.

"My old boss, Gunner. He has a computer expert for me."

"Great." He cleared his throat. "About last night . . . I'm sorry I put you through that."

Duke barked at the back door, and I let him back into the house. "Seriously, there's no reason to apologize."

Brad studied my face, "How are you feeling?"

My head still throbbed, and I was reeling from the previous evening's raw emotions and lack of sleep. "Fine." Duke yipped.

"Are you sure you feel up to working today? Maybe you should rest."

"Honest, I'm fine." Duke yipped again.

"What's the matter with your dog?"

"Dunno. Maybe it's the new surroundings?" That earned another yip.

Brad squinted and then glanced back and forth between my dog and me. "Wait a minute." He stopped and studied my face. I couldn't look him in the eyes. "Wow, sure is pouring rain outside."

Since the sun was streaming through the kitchen windows, of course, my dog yipped again. "We're in Charleston," Brad added. Another yip. "And Liz is lying." No yip.

Brad groaned. "When were you planning to tell me about his lie-detector abilities?" He placed the water bottle down and crossed his arms.

I sank into the kitchen chair and explained, "It's his super power. I discovered it not long after I got him. He helps me with investigations. That's one reason why I want to bring him along when I do the employee interviews."

"Yeah. But why wouldn't you tell me?" He shook his head. "Were you hoping to use it against me? Please don't tell me you think I'm the one behind the thefts."

"No, of course not."

"Well, I'm comforted that your dog didn't yip. But I'm disappointed that you kept this from me." He took a step back.

While I massaged Duke's ears, I wondered how this was going to work now that we both knew his abilities. Would we constantly be testing each other in front of my dog? Would Brad even want to continue the relationship? My heart sank.

"I need to take a walk." He exited the back door without another word.

When he returned fifteen minutes later, he said, "We need to figure out this Duke thing at some point. But not this morning. I have a meeting."

"OK." I hadn't moved since he left. "Please don't tell anyone about his abilities. Peg was the only other person who knew. Until now."

He grimaced. "Of course, I'd never tell."

Brad opened a kitchen drawer and grabbed a set of car keys. "These are for the Mercedes. Do you remember how to get to the office?"

"I think so." I hesitated. "Do you have another car I can use?" I'd no idea how much the Mercedes cost. It looked expensive. After yesterday's experience, I was wary.

He chuckled, and the tension in the room dissipated. "You think this is a rental place?" Fumbling in the drawer, he fished out another set of keys. "How about the Mustang?"

"That's better. Thank you."

"Hey, I have an idea. Come on."

I followed Brad out the kitchen door to the backyard. Duke dashed in front of us to search for squirrels.

"The guest house has a nice office you can use. It's where Peg stayed when she visited."

Some of my research needed to be conducted away from MultiPoint's offices. A spot where I could set up shop would be perfect.

He turned the key in the door and flipped on the lights. The guest house was decorated in soft creams and hues of blues. We navigated through the combined kitchen, family room, and dining area and made our way to a hallway that led to a bedroom, bathroom, office, and small laundry room. I could envision Peg in this space.

"Peg decorated?" It was more of a statement than a question. Her touch was everywhere.

"Of course." Brad motioned to the room on the right. "Here's the office."

A built-in desk and bookcase faced wall-to-wall windows that overlooked the Pacific Ocean. I surveyed the room and smiled. "Not too shabby."

He flipped on the lights. "There should be bottled water and some drinks in the fridge, and of course, you're welcome to help yourself to anything in the house."

"Um, do you mind if I remove some of the artwork from the walls?" Paintings of Carmel By-the-Sea covered the two walls facing each other.

He shrugged. "No problem. I guess you can stuff them in one of the closets. Why?"

"I'd like to put up a whiteboard and a cork board. I couldn't imagine trying to solve a case without them. Is there an office supply store close by?"

"Yes." Brad grabbed a notepad off the desk and jotted down directions to the closest shop. "Hammer and nails are on a shelf in the garage."

"And a grocery store? I want to make you dinner for your birthday."

His eyes brightened, and he grinned dimple to dimple. "*That* will go a long way to make up for this morning. Whatcha cooking?" he asked as he wrote down the second set of directions.

"Surprise."

"If it's anything like the last meal you cooked for me, I can hardly wait."

I smiled at the memory of Brad devouring the King Ranch chicken dinner I'd served him in Charleston.

He tore off the page and handed me his notes.

"Well, better get going." He leaned in to kiss me goodbye. Bathed in the warmth of the sunlight, we kissed for nearly a minute before Brad pulled away. "If we keep at it, I'll miss my meeting."

~ * ~

After unpacking the groceries, I glanced at the time on the microwave oven. Noon. I shot off a quick text to Brad.

> Not going to make it to the office. Errands took longer than expected.

I fixed myself a turkey sandwich, placed a couple of extra slices of cheese on the plate for Duke, and made my way to the guesthouse. After I set my lunch on the desk, I began making the office space my own while my dog patiently guarded the cheese. Once the cork board and whiteboard were hung, I sat down to eat and rewarded Duke with a piece of cheese. I opened the first folder and grabbed a dry-erase marker. Somehow, Tim had managed to get bank information on the new identities. As I reviewed the documents, I determined the thieves had the same MO. They opened a bank account. Then using the debit card, the perps ordered prescriptions online. The orders appeared to be on auto-renewal. I looked up the company, RXFast, and wondered if I could find out the names of the prescribing doctors.

Between bites of my sandwich, I began outlining the details of each case.

Identity Theft Victim 1 (Tim's friend)

Age 42, single, no kids
Monterey Vista, CA 1421 Canyon Way
Died of a heart attack early December last year
Service with MultiPoint canceled in February

Synthetic Identity 1

Age 42
San Jose, CA Paradise Apartments #323
Bank Account – Secure Bank
Prescription orders for Oxycodone and Ritalin through RXFast

Identity Theft Victim 2

Age 60
Alta Mesa, CA 1022 Sunset Drive
Divorced, no kids
Service with MultiPoint canceled in March

Synthetic Identity 2

Age 60
San Jose, CA Meadow Brook Apartments #107
Bank Account – Community Bank
Prescription orders for Oxycodone and Valium through RXFast

Identity Theft Victim 3

Age 30
New Monterey, CA Cedar Ridge Apartments #23B
Air Force, Deployed to Iraq
Single, no kids
Service with MultiPoint canceled in April

Synthetic Identity 3

Age 30
San Jose, CA Galaxy Apartments #201
Bank Account – Secure Bank
Prescription orders for Xanax and Ritalin through RXFast
Service with MultiPoint canceled in May

Identity Theft Victim 4

Age 70
Villa Del Monte, CA 225 North Oaks
Widowed
Service with MultiPoint canceled in June

Synthetic Identity 4

Age 75
San Jose, CA Crestwood Apartments #235
Bank Account – Community Bank
Prescription orders for Oxycodone and Xanax through RXFast

I handed Duke the last piece of cheese and stood back to examine the board. All the victims were in the Monterey area. I briefly wondered if foul play was involved in their deaths. "Nah, that'd alert the authorities," I muttered. Turning on my laptop, I Googled each victim's name and searched for their obituary. I knew Tim's friend had died of a sudden, massive heart attack. The second victim had died in a tragic car accident. The airman in the Air Force died while on duty. The widower had passed peacefully in his sleep. All the victims were male. I made a note to review the records to see if any other cancellations due to death had occurred since the start of the year.

Next, I turned my attention to the synthetic identities. As I Googled each apartment address, I jotted down the leasing office contact information. All of the apartments were on the southeast side of the city and were within a fifteen-mile radius. I called each of them and pretended to be interested in renting a place. The application process could be done online, and the deposit was minimal. A trip to San Jose was definitely on the horizon.

Duke pawed my leg. Yikes, it was already 2:00. "Go for a walk, boy?"

He bounded toward the door.

When we returned from our walk, I glanced at a message on my phone.

> In and out of meetings all day. Missed you. Meet up for cocktails at 5:30? Sunsets Bar and Grille has a great happy hour.

Brad had included a link with directions.

I replied.

> See you there.

Pulling out the employee index cards I'd created and the organizational chart Tim gave me, I began pinning the index cards to the cork board according to reporting lines. I'd never get all one hundred-plus employees on the board, but I was getting a solid visual of the company. As I studied the board, I determined that the customer service team was as decent a place as any to start the interviews. I needed to get the VPs on board first. I spent the next half hour arranging tomorrow's meetings with the three VPs.

My phone pinged with a text from my neighbor, Linda.

> Hello love, hope you're having fun. Are you coming Saturday? Trivia. Will be fun!!

Our Charleston neighborhood had a game night on the second Saturday of each month. It was Linda's turn to host. Since she'd been out of town last week, we'd postponed until this Saturday.

> Wouldn't miss it!

I hit send, closed the blinds, and headed to the house to freshen up before driving to Sunsets.

Chapter 10

The sun beamed in a cloudless sky. A soft breeze blew through the compound. It was another rainless day. Peanut adjusted the dark green gardening apron. Today's t-shirt was a bright cherry red. He felt like a Christmas card. At least the darker-colored garment would make it more difficult to spot him when he decided to bolt. This morning, he was confined to the greenhouse. After lunch, he'd water the south side of the garden and search for a way to escape.

He picked the plump ruby tomatoes off the vine, placed them in a basket, and hummed a tune, "King of the Road," one of his favorites by Roger Miller. Cameras were positioned in each corner of the large glass structure. The location of the exits would make it difficult to leave without being spotted by the cameras. Two other men picked various vegetables and fruits, leafy kale, green beans, strawberries, watermelon, and peppers in every color and size. Both men were Members. Peanut was the sole Newbie. Although conversation was discouraged, he decided to take advantage of his Newbie status and quiz the Member with the longest tenure.

"Hey Jack, can you help me out here?"

"Whatcha need?"

"I ain't sure these tomatoes are ripe enough to pick."

Jack walked over and examined the tomatoes in question. Cupping a tomato in the palm of his hand, he said, "This one here needs a little more time on the vine. Notice the bit of green on the top. Also, it's too firm. There should be a bit of give but not too soft." He demonstrated by pressing on the fruit.

"Gotcha. How long did it take you to figure all this stuff out?"

"Not long. You'll learn." He gently dropped the tomato and wiped his palms on his apron.

"Hey, those cameras work?"

Jack took a step back and studied Peanut's face.

"I don't wanna get in trouble or nothing for talking to you is all."

"Yes. Now get back to work."

"Yes sir."

Lunch was a hearty meal of fried chicken, mashed potatoes, and green beans. Peanut sat at a long cafeteria-style table with the other garden workers and a designated Disciple. As he shoveled food in his mouth, he avoided speaking. He definitely didn't want to stand out in the crowd. Some of the older Members made small talk about the weather or this evening's service. Ho-hum. So boring. He was ready to get back outdoors.

The temperature had warmed a good ten degrees since sunrise. The dark green baseball cap offered some protection from the scorching sun. Peanut adjusted his hat, picked up the spray hose, and began watering the carrots. A small grove of orange, lemon, and lime trees lined the fence. No one had provided any instruction on what he should or shouldn't water, so he headed there next.

The concrete fence was crowned with barbed wire. Didn't look like he'd be climbing over, too risky anyway. A tool shed backed up against the fence. He imagined it held tractors, mowers, and other gardening gear. To the left was a gate. As he sprayed water on the roots of the trees, Peanut peered around before moving closer. He spewed cuss words under his breath when he ran out of hose length. He couldn't tell from here what type of lock was on the gate, but it looked like a promising way out. His mind spun as he tried to determine how he could get a better view. The Disciple in charge of the gardens came marching toward him. Holy mackerel. He hoped he wasn't in trouble. No telling what they did to disobedient Newbies.

"You still know how to operate a tractor?" the Disciple asked.

Peanut had worked in construction before he took to the streets. "You betcha. Like riding a bike. Nevah forget."

"One of my tractor guys fell and cracked a couple of ribs. I'll need you to dig some new beds for me tomorrow."

"You got it, boss." Looked like he just got lucky. Access to a tractor provided all kinds of possibilities. Yup, it was only a matter of time before he'd bust this joint.

~ * ~

Apollo fumed. The nerve of that woman. She never even half considered donating her property to the Mission. Even though he'd given her an hour tour and showed her all the good he was doing. He'd originally hoped that the THC-laced cookie would've gotten her pulled over and arrested. Not his best move. The last thing he needed was drugs linked to the Mission. He needed to be more careful. Her sudden appearance had thrown him off balance. His mind spun as he considered other options.

Perhaps if he built another underground warehouse, with enough time he could purchase the property himself. He made a note to run the numbers. That foreign company paid him handsomely to store the black-market drugs.

He needed to keep closer tabs on Liz and Brad. Extracting a couple of file folders from his desk drawer, he created a file for each of them and placed the form they'd completed inside. "Get Cosmo," he hollered to wife number two.

"What's up, boss?" Cosmo entered and sat in one of the two chairs in front of the desk.

Apollo slid the folders over. "Find out everything you can on these two. Print out anything you discover and put it in the folder. I want articles, pictures, past addresses, names of family and friends." He slapped his hand on the desk. "Even their underwear sizes."

Cosmo jumped. "You got it, boss." He grabbed the folders and quickly exited. He didn't dare ask any questions.

Chapter 11

Brad waved at me from a table outside. I'd had no trouble finding the place, but parking was a challenge. I was fifteen minutes late.

"Sorry, I'm late."

He stood and pulled out a chair for me. "I was just about to call you. How are you feeling?"

"One hundred percent better."

Brad hesitated over the back of my chair, and an awkward moment passed between us. "Dang, this no public display of affection is going to be hard. You look fantastic." He returned to his chair.

"Thank you." The butterflies in my stomach fluttered in response to the compliment. I picked up the menu and averted his gaze. I felt awkward after last night, and this morning's discovery of my dog's abilities only added to my unease. Perusing the list of wines by the glass, I selected the house chardonnay and gave my order to the waiter.

Once the waiter was out of earshot, Brad leaned forward and said, "We need to talk about Duke."

I fidgeted in my seat. "OK."

"We can't use his lie-detecting skills against each other."

I picked imaginary lint off my floral blouse. "OK."

"Liz. Look at me. I'm serious."

I raised my face and looked him in the eye.

He continued, "I get that there may be times when we don't want to answer a question. But no lying to each other. If either one of us needs space, we say so."

"I can live with that . . ." I chewed my lower lip while Brad waited patiently for me to continue. "It's just . . . I'm so used to his abilities. Asking questions and listening to Duke's reaction . . . it's a hard habit to break."

He leaned back in his chair.

"And I can't help it. Sometimes I blurt out a little white lie."

Brad's face softened, and he laughed. "Little white lies are fine. It's the big ones that'll get us in trouble."

I contemplated my new reality. "Maybe we could have some fun with it. Like put five bucks in a jar every time one of us lies. Or asks a question we shouldn't."

"Or something else instead of money." He winked.

The server interrupted with my glass of wine, and I took a long sip of the buttery liquid while my red face returned to normal.

I changed the subject. "I booked meetings with each of your VPs tomorrow. I need to get them on board."

"Probably wise. Let me know if you need me to be there."

"Thanks." I filled him in on my whiteboard and cork board handiwork. I added, "I'm also going to hire a computer expert."

"Sounds reasonable."

"I want to see if they can obtain the name of the prescribing doctor." I paused, "And I want them to try to hack your computer systems."

He crossed his arms in front of his chest and said, "I really think that's a waste of time and money. Our systems are airtight. I'd be shocked if this is a hack job."

"Of course, they are," I reassured him, "but it won't hurt to confirm it."

Brad reached for his glass and swirled the ice in his scotch. "OK. Is this the name Gunner gave you?"

"Yes. If you want, I can run his credentials by you tomorrow." A cool breeze blew off the ocean. An early evening fog began to roll in. I pulled my denim jacket tighter around my chest.

"No need. I trust you."

I breathed a sigh of relief. I'd hoped he wouldn't micromanage every step of the way.

He picked up the happy hour menu. "How about we get a couple of appetizers to share? It's plenty of food. What about the sliders and the crab cakes?"

"Works for me."

Brad placed our order, adding an order of calamari and a garden salad with balsamic vinaigrette dressing on the side.

I wondered if I should bring up his nightmare from the previous night. A few moments of silence passed, and I decided it'd be better to let him share more when he was ready. Instead, I asked, "Do you have to change your diet when the triathlon gets closer?"

"I usually lay off the alcohol a few days before and increase my protein intake. That's about it."

"Oh. I forgot to mention that I think I might need to visit San Jose."

"When?"

"When I get back."

His eyes brightened. "Maybe I can join you? We could stay overnight and visit a winery. I hate that you're not getting a vacation."

"I don't know if that's a good plan. I'll spend at least half of my time in a car doing surveillance work."

Giving me his best puppy-dog face, he said, "Please? I'll get Alice to book us a suite at the Hayes."

I shook my head, "Bad idea." I held up a finger, "One, how do you know she isn't in on this?"

"Impossible—"

"No assumptions at this point." I added a second finger. "And two, this is a working trip. Not a fun jaunt to San Jose."

"OK. You do your surveillance thing, and I'll stay at the hotel and work while you're gone." He grinned. " Then you'll have me to come back to after a long, hard day."

"What about Duke?"

"I bet Tim would watch him."

I couldn't help but smile. "I'll think about it."

Our appetizers arrived. I added a crab cake to my plate. After I dipped a bite of crab into the mustard sauce, I savored the flavors of the sweet meat combined with the tart sauce. "Delicious."

"Wait till you try the calamari."

"So . . ." I studied Brad's face for a moment before continuing. "You have any enemies?"

"What kind of question is that?"

"A valid one. Who would want you or your company to fail?" I stabbed a piece of calamari with my fork. The outside was crunchy, the inside tender. "Mmm."

He sipped his scotch as he pondered the question. "Ted Oliver." He spat the name out. "He's the CEO of SecureLife. Been in business longer than us. We've taken some of their market share." Sinking his teeth into a slider, he ate for a moment then added, "I was at a conference about two years ago. He and I were supposed to be on a panel together. I ended up getting violently ill. I swear he slipped something into my drink at the dinner table. No one else had any issues."

I reached into my purse, pulled out my notebook, and started taking notes.

"You want some of this salad?" I nodded, and Brad divided the salad between our plates and passed the dressing.

"Who else?"

"Maybe Chandler Price? We're not enemies, just fierce competitors in the triathlon world." He shook his head. "Nah, he might like it if I was distracted, but I can't imagine him going to that kind of extreme. It'd be much easier to mess with my bike."

I jotted down the name anyway. "Any ex-girlfriends or jilted lovers?"

"Is this a clever ploy to learn about my love life?"

My face grew warm despite the cool breeze. "Absolutely not," I protested. "Names only. No need for any details." This path of the investigation was uncomfortable with a capital U. There was a reason for the 'not getting involved with a client' rule. Although, I had to admit a part of me wanted the lowdown.

"I was involved with a woman in college. She dropped me. Not the other way around. I've dated plenty since then but nothing serious."

"Tell me about the woman in college."

"Teresa? I don't see how she's relevant. Like I said, she's the one who broke it off."

"Anybody else? Someone who might've thought the relationship was something more than you did?"

He rested his chin in his palm and chewed on his lower lip as he pondered the question. "There was Sally. We didn't date, but she was kind of obsessed with me."

"Who's Sally?"

"Sally Anderson. She was my assistant before Alice. She practically stalked me. We tried to transfer her to a different department. In the end, we let her go. That was years ago."

"You didn't mention her before."

"It's been so long, I forgot about her. I heard she's married now with a couple of kids."

"Still lives in the area?"

He shrugged. "No idea."

Definitely a lead worth pursuing.

~ * ~

Last night we'd relaxed on Brad's deck and watched the sun set over the Pacific. While Duke hunted for lizards in the container pots, the sun sank, casting soft orange and peach hues on the fog-tinged sky.

Brad broke the silence. "You asked about Teresa. My relationship with her isn't relevant to the investigation, but since the breakup still stings, I might as well tell you."

I tilted my head toward him. Great, just what I needed . . . the girlfriend he never got over. His expression looked pained.

"We dated in high school. USC wasn't my first choice . . . it was so far away from my parents. But I followed her there. Our sophomore year, she dumped me for a guy I thought was a friend." He closed his eyes. "She broke my heart, but that wasn't the worst part."

I waited for him to continue.

"That first year, I didn't go home for the summer. My mom practically begged me. I'd hoped that maybe if I stuck around Teresa might change her mind . . . and then, like that, my parents were gone."

Oh my God. I made a mental note to call my mom and dad tomorrow. "Brad, I don't know what to say. That must have been awful."

He shook his head. "I don't know why I'm telling you all of this, I'm over her. Maybe I just want you to understand."

"What do you mean?" I tugged on my earring.

"Creating MultiPoint, competing in the triathlons. It's all part of what gave me new meaning to life."

Yikes, the pressure to solve the case had just intensified. The temperature dropped as the sky became darker. I shivered. "Why don't we go inside?"

Back indoors, we promptly made up for the earlier restrained display of affection.

~ * ~

Over breakfast, I'd promised Brad that I would stop by his office as soon as I arrived. On the drive in, I'd called my parents and told them I loved them.

My heart fluttered as I walked toward his office. I'd left Duke behind. Later, I planned to bring him along for the employee interviews and put his lie-detector skills to the test. Brad was on the phone, so I turned my focus to his assistant. "Good morning, Alice."

She lifted her perfectly manicured hands from the keyboard and gave me her full attention. "Good morning. You look well-rested."

My face flushed. "Thank you." I blew on the mug of hot tea I'd brewed in the common kitchen. "So, how long have you worked for Brad?" I knew the answer, but it was an easy place to start a bit of sleuthing.

"Six years. He's a wonderful boss." She clasped her hands together and smiled. Her brown eyes twinkled behind the lenses of her glasses.

After a sip of my tea, I placed the mug on the counter of her cubicle. "Six years is a long time. Have there ever been any tough periods?"

She straightened her spine, and huffed, "Never."

It wasn't going to be easy prying the office dirt out of her. I changed the subject, "Are you from California?"

"No. Originally from upstate New York. I've been here for thirty years. And you?"

"Atlanta, but I've been in Charleston for a while." I glanced in Brad's direction. He was still on the phone. "Moving here must've been quite the climate change for you."

She adjusted her spectacles. "Sure was, but I don't miss the winters."

Perched next to a pot of succulents were several framed photos. I pointed to one of the pictures and asked, "Is that your family?" There were at least fifty people in the photo.

She picked up the frame and handed it to me. "Yes. This one is from last year's family reunion. I try to make it every year."

"You have a big family."

She beamed. "Everyone who has the last name Stanistreet is related. Most of us are in New York, but there are a few in California, Nevada, Florida, England, and even Australia."

"You're lucky. I'm an only child. My parents each had one sibling. We might have eight people at our family gatherings." I handed the picture back to her.

She motioned toward Brad's office. "Looks like he's off the phone."

"Thanks, Alice." I picked up my tea and walked his way.

After I'd checked in with Brad, I settled into Tim's office and reviewed the records to see if there were any other cancellations of services due to death. Finding none, I spent the rest of the morning meeting with two of the three VPs. Confident I had their support, I began to list the people I needed to interview. Brad had lunch plans, so I joined the employees in the common area. No pets were allowed in this space. I could only imagine the chaos that would ensue if they were permitted.

After I picked up a boxed meal of chicken tenders with shoestring fries, I searched for an empty seat. I spotted two empty spots at a table with a woman whom I'd met yesterday, and a guy I didn't recognize. "Mind if I join you, Zelda?"

She glanced at her table mate and hesitated before she answered, "Not at all. Um, Bryce, this is Liz. She's a consultant."

"Nice to meet you. Do you work for MultiPoint?" I was confident I hadn't met him before. His olive complexion, tawny brown eyes, and slightly receding jet-black hair slicked back with some kind of man product were memorable.

"No, I'm here to do the quarterly audit." He slid his chair back an inch from the table.

From the clipped tone of his voice, I got the impression he wasn't too happy I'd joined them.

"Bryce is an external auditor. He's been working for us for—how many years?" she asked Bryce.

"Five." He turned his attention toward me, narrowing his eyes. "What kind of consulting do you do?"

"Process improvement. I'm here to review MultiPoint's processes and find ways to improve the workflow."

He studied my face. Zelda broke the silence, "Liz is a family friend of Brad's."

As I dipped a chicken tender into the honey mustard sauce, I continued, "I'd be interested in your ideas since you've worked with the company for so long."

"All I do is look at the numbers. I don't have any suggestions for you." He wiped his hands on a napkin and picked up the remnants of his lunch. "See you later, Z." Nodding at me, he said, "Nice to meet you, Liz."

"I hope I didn't offend him."

Zelda squirmed in her chair. "I don't think so. He's a typical numbers guy. Kinda keeps to himself." She picked up her empty box. "I hate to leave you, but I need to get back to work."

"No worries. You go ahead." I noticed that she headed in the same direction as Bryce . . . the opposite direction of her workspace.

Back at my desk after a lonely lunch, I asked Tim to tell me what he knew about Zelda and Bryce.

"Zelda's a pretty private person. Never been married, she lives with her mother. She's a very conscientious employee." Irish jumped up on his desk. Tim rubbed the cat's back as he continued. "Bryce is a professional. Does a good job with the audit. I don't know much about him beyond that. Both of them are smokers. Neither one of them stay long at company social events." Irish purred with contentment. "Why do you ask?"

"Just curious. I ate lunch at their table."

We both worked in comfortable silence for a little while longer, then I broke the quiet with a question. "So? What's it like working for Brad?"

"It's been great. We built this company together from the ground up. We've had our moments. But I couldn't ask for a better business partner." He hesitated before he continued," I'm trying to convince him now is the right time to sell."

"You're thinking of selling?" That was a shock. I couldn't imagine Brad putting the company up for sale.

Tim ran his hand along Irish's back. "Maybe. Of course, we need to get this mess resolved first."

"What do you like to do for fun?" I enjoyed getting to know Tim better. His easy-going demeanor was the opposite of most CFOs I'd met, and his affection for his cat was endearing.

"I write. So far, only short stories, but I'd love to write a full-length novel if I had the time."

"I'm an avid reader. What kind of short stories?" I asked.

"Thrillers for the most part. Although, I hope to write some children's books about Irish."

"Cool. I'd love to read them if you're willing to share."

"I've had one published in a magazine. I'll bring you a copy."

"I can't wait to read it." I turned my attention back toward work and opened an email from Gunner with the computer contact, Lawson James. Wait—I knew the name, Peg's niece's boyfriend. I remembered Jenny mentioning that he worked with computers, but I thought he worked for one of those IT service companies. When I placed the call, I confirmed he was indeed Jenny's friend. He did consulting work on the side. He explained that his company was OK with it. I detailed the scope of the project to him, and he promised to deliver a proposal with costs by the end of the day.

Satisfied that item was taken care of, I scheduled meetings for next week with the people on the list of employees I'd identified earlier. I looked forward to bringing Duke along. With thirty minutes to spare before my meeting with the VP of Operations, I Googled SecureLife and Ted Oliver.

I took an instant dislike to the image of Ted I saw on the website. He had a bulbous nose and a bald head. Otherwise, he wasn't bad looking, even though his eyes were beady, and his smile looked forced. SecureLife was a public company, and the stock had floundered the last few quarters due to lower-than-expected earnings. He must be under a lot of pressure to boost the bottom line. Perhaps I could persuade him to meet with me by offering consulting services designed to improve revenues and reduce expenses. If I shared that MultiPoint was also a client his interest might be piqued.

Or I could work the female angle. He was recently divorced. I wondered where he liked to hang out. As I scanned a few articles, a plan formulated. At lunchtime, he liked to walk his dogs along the trails that bordered the company. I penciled a visit to SecureLife into my schedule.

Chapter 12

Landing the tractor gig was a dream come true. As soon as he walked into the shed to retrieve the vehicle, Peanut began to devise a plan of escape. The backside of the shed had a long narrow window he was confident he could squeeze through. When he wasn't being supervised so closely, he'd climb on a piece of equipment and check it out. He turned the key in the ignition and put the tractor in gear. The sound of the motor drowned out his thoughts as he made his way to the section of land where he'd dig the new beds.

After a morning of shoveling dirt, Peanut returned the tractor to the shed. He'd noticed the cameras on the front of the shed, but there didn't appear to be any on the inside. Confident no one was watching, he climbed on the tractor underneath the window and peered outside. Through the grimy glass, he spotted several large oak trees on the other side of the fence. It'd be simple enough to slip out the window, hoist himself onto the roof, and climb a tree to the other side. If he had some rope, the task would be much easier.

Peanut climbed down, dusted his palms on the front of his apron, and looked around. Sure enough, there was a coil of rope in the far corner of the shed. He quickly exited, closed the doors, and secured the padlock. It'd be easy enough to pick the lock when the time was right. He strode toward the cafeteria to join the others for lunch.

As he walked, he contemplated how, and when, he'd make his escape. Not broad daylight. Too risky. Slipping out of the barracks in the night would be tough. Cameras monitored every move inside most of the buildings. His mind replayed his initial tour of the compound. He pulled off his cap and wiped the sweat off his forehead. The sick bay. No one seemed to want those jobs. When they toured the facility, the building was lightly staffed. He couldn't remember the locations of the cameras, but he'd figure it out. All he had to do was fake an illness. He picked up the pace with a spring in his step. It was only a matter of time.

~ * ~

Apollo stretched out his legs on the leather ottoman in his personal living quarters. The glossy black walls adorned with gilded mirrors eased his anxiety. Cosmo had delivered his findings on the couple earlier. Comforted by the space he called home, Apollo contemplated his options as he smoked a joint. Play it nice and go for the CEO's bucks or remove that woman from the picture? Perhaps both? It was time to step up the game and gather some first-hand information. He'd brief Cosmo later.

He summoned wife number two. The Members were discouraged from having sexual relations, but not Apollo. Tonight was her lucky night.

Chapter 13

Up early, I attempted to work the coffee maker before Brad awoke. Today was Brad's birthday, and I was determined to greet him with a cup of joe. Pressing the brew button, I inhaled the rich aroma of dark roast. My body clock had adjusted to Pacific Time, just in time for my trip back to Charleston. Yesterday's conversation with the VP of Operations proved fruitful. I'd learned a lot about the inner workings of the company. Other than a side trip to SecureLife and Brad's former assistant's home, I'd be holed up in the guest house for most of the day. Before I left, I wanted to prep tonight's lasagna casserole and bake the cherry almond birthday cake.

After I gave Duke his breakfast, I poured two cups of coffee. I needed the extra fuel.

"Happy Birthday." I handed the steaming mug to Brad and climbed into bed next to him.

"Please tell me you're not going to sing."

I could actually sing, but Brad had witnessed me imitating Peg singing karaoke. She couldn't carry a tune. "Ha. Don't worry. I'll spare you." I stretched my toes toward the end of the bed. "What time do you have to be in the office?"

Brad grinned. "What'd you have in mind?"

I set my coffee mug down on the nightstand and demonstrated exactly what I had in mind.

~ * ~

After I prepped the lasagna, I divided the casserole, placing half in the fridge and the other half in the freezer. I smiled. Something for Brad to remember me by. The cake cooled on the counter. I'd ice it when I returned. Curled in his dog bed, Duke softly snored, content from eating the remnants of ground beef from the pan. Satisfied everything was in good order for this evening's celebration, I left for SecureLife.

Tucked in my purse was a photo of MultiPoint's former employee, Mitch. If I spotted him, I would take advantage of the opportunity to talk to him. The offices were further inland, close to the airport. The building was a modern concrete structure with dark glass windows. A horseshoe hike and bike trail surrounded the business. I parked Brad's Mustang in a visitor's slot and headed toward the entrance of the trail. Lined with picnic tables, the space was lushly landscaped with greenery, bright red and pink roses, and blue hydrangeas. Conversation buzzed in the air as employees ate their lunches. Cloud cover and a breeze offered some relief from the mid-day sun.

I immediately spotted a man who looked a lot like Ted Oliver walking two Jack Russell terriers a few yards ahead. I hurried to catch up.

"What adorable dogs. Do you mind if I pet them?"

He looked me up and down appreciatively. I wore a white linen V-neck blouse with khaki capris and white leather Keds. The neckline dipped just enough to show off a little cleavage.

"Go ahead. They're friendly."

I bent down and scratched their heads. "Hi, guys." I looked back up at Ted. "What are their names?"

"Par and Birdie."

"Cute. You must be a golfer."

"I am. And you are?"

I stood back up and offered my hand. "Liz. And not a golfer." A throaty laugh escaped my lips as I tossed my blonde hair over my shoulder.

"Pleasure to meet you. I'm Ted Oliver, CEO of SecureLife." He shook my hand then stood back and studied my face. "I don't recognize you. Are you a new employee?"

"Oh my, I'm so sorry. Is this private property?" I slid my sunglasses off and placed them on top of my head. "I'm visiting. I was driving around and needed to stretch my legs."

"It's OK. I'm glad you stopped." He gazed into my eyes. "Where are you visiting from?"

"South Carolina." I averted my gaze to my sneakers and made a quick decision to work the female angle. "I'm recently divorced. I had to get far away to some place where no one knew me for a while. I've always wanted to see the California coast."

"How long are you here for?"

When I looked back up, I smiled coyly. "Indefinitely."

He reached into his pocket and pulled out a business card. "I'd love to show you around. Call this number and give my assistant your contact information."

"Oh. I couldn't possibly impose." The Russells danced around my feet.

"It would be my pleasure," he replied, reining his dogs in.

"Thank you. I'd like that."

"I have a full weekend. Maybe Monday or Tuesday night next week? I could take you to a couple of my favorite spots downtown."

He glanced at the time on his phone. "I've gotta run to a meeting. See you soon, Liz."

"Looking forward to it." I watched him stride toward the front entrance with Par and Birdie in tow. *Score.*

Now if I could only be as lucky with my next stop today. I popped into a fast food restaurant to change into a more conservative shirt.

Sally lived in a neighborhood not far from SecureLife. I parked the Mustang on a side street and walked up Story Street. Her mission-style home was halfway to the top of the hill. In my online research, I'd discovered that after she'd left MultiPoint she'd married and had two kids. She was now a full-time stay-at-home mom. Clipboard in hand, I strode up to her front door and rang the doorbell.

A pretty woman with a long brunette ponytail answered the door. A young boy about four stood behind her and hugged her leg.

"Good afternoon, I wonder if you'd have some time for a quick survey?" I claimed to be with the Democratic Party, even though I was a staunch Republican. I'd printed the questions off the California Democratic Party website before I left Brad's place. "It won't take more than ten minutes of your time." I expected to have the door slammed in my face, so I was surprised when she invited me in.

"I'm Liz, and you are?" I bent down to shake the boy's hand.

"This is Noah, and I'm Sally. Let's go to the kitchen." I followed Sally down the hallway. "The baby is sleeping. I'm surprised the doorbell didn't wake her."

"Oh, dear. I'm glad I didn't disturb her."

"It's OK. Interruptions are the story of my life. Follow me."

Sally pulled a pitcher of ice-cold lemonade from the fridge and set a couple of glasses on the kitchen table. "Please help yourself." She added a plate of oatmeal cookies.

As I poured the cool liquid into the glass, I started with small talk. "How long have you lived here?"

She settled Noah into a booster seat and handed him a tumbler of lemonade and a cookie. "Almost five years. My husband and I moved in when we were expecting Noah."

"Seems like a nice neighborhood."

She sat next to her son. "It is. If you don't mind, can we get started on the survey?"

"Of course." I jotted down the basics, her full name, her age, her gender, and her race. "Occupation?"

"Stay-at-home mom."

"Did you ever work?"

"Yes, before I got married. Since then there's been no need and the kids keep me very busy."

"What did you do?"

She shrugged. "I was an executive assistant. I worked for my husband, Phil. That's how we met." Smiling, she picked up a napkin and dabbed at Noah's cookie-covered lips.

She was either a very good actor, or she truly was as happy as she appeared. After we completed the survey questions, I placed my empty glass next to the sink and mentally dropped her to the bottom of the suspect list.

I was back in the office at Brad's guest house by three. While Duke basked in the sun outside, I added notes to index cards. I drew a long vertical line down the whiteboard next to the identity theft victims. At the top of the space, I wrote <u>Suspects</u>. The first one on the list was Ted Oliver. I then listed Mitch, Sally, and Chandler Price. Out to the side of Sally and Chandler, I added "long shot." The list wasn't very long, but I was only getting started. I glanced at the time, nearly four. I needed to pack a few things for my return trip to Charleston tomorrow, ice the cake, put the lasagna in the oven, and get ready for the evening. After dinner, we were going out on the town. I closed the blinds, locked the door, and headed back to the main house with my dog at my heels.

~ * ~

The limo driver dropped us off at Clint Eastwood's old bar, The Hog's Breath Inn. I secretly hoped for a Clint sighting. Brad raved about my lasagna and the cherry almond cake the whole trip. My jeans felt a little snug, and I was ready to work off dinner on the dance floor. While Brad ordered our drinks at the bar, I snagged a table close to the stage.

The corners of my mouth dropped when Brad returned not only with our cocktails but also with Sam and another woman. "Look who I found. You don't mind if Sam and her friend join us, do you?"

"I didn't know it was Brad's birthday," Sam commented. "This is my friend, Rosie. She's visiting from Louisiana."

My Southern inner bitch and Southern hostess fought with each other before I replied, "Have a seat." Sam was dressed in a black sleeveless top and white jeans. The hammered silver jewelry accented her tan. Her friend Rosie's skin was a creamy Cajun latte. Her long auburn hair framed emerald eyes. Ms. Sexy and Ms. Stunning had just joined us. Nice. I leaned back in my chair and crossed my arms. "How long are you visiting, Rosie?"

"For the long weekend." She sat in the seat on the other side of Brad. "*Laissez les bons temps rouler.*" Rosie raised her glass. "Happy Birthday to Brad."

"Cheers." We all clinked our drinks.

"Might be the best birthday ever." Brad didn't seem the least bit uncomfortable being surrounded by women. I had to admit it. I was jealous.

As the band tested the equipment and sound, Rosie entertained us with Boudreaux and Thibodeaux jokes. Those two

Cajun characters were legendary and quite funny. I was starting to like the woman.

"Brad, I call dibs on the first dance," Sam said.

"Well, bless your heart, Sam. I don't think so," I responded.

Rosie sputtered her beer out and laughed.

"What?" Sam asked bewildered.

Brad sat silent unsure where this was headed. I winked at Rosie sharing the Southern joke. Saying "bless your heart" with a slight Southern lilt was the ultimate insult. The band started the first set with the Beach Boys' "California Girls."

Rosie walked around Brad's chair, grabbed my hand and Sam's hand, and pulled us out onto the dance floor. The next song up was Kool and the Gang's "Celebration." Rosie started to recruit other dancers from the crowd. She was a band's dream. Sam and I bumped our butts and attempted to see how low we could go. I wiggled a little extra for Brad's benefit. My thighs would be sore tomorrow. Feeling bad for leaving Brad by himself, I sat the next song out.

The band switched to a slow melody, Berlin's "Take My Breath Away." Brad grabbed my hand. "Dance?"

I nodded, and we walked hand in hand onto the dance floor. As I settled into his body, we swayed to the rhythm. My ex was an awful dancer. At our wedding reception, we'd nearly tripped over each other during the first dance. Brad was smooth, and it felt like I'd been dancing with him all my life. I raised my head off his chest and commented, "This band is really good."

He leaned forward and whispered in my ear. "Sometimes, I look at you, and I can't breathe." My heart skipped a few beats. "You are one beautiful woman, Liz Adams."

I wanted the song to last forever.

The music changed, and Brad reluctantly released the embrace. As we walked off the dance floor, I glanced toward the bar and spotted Zelda and Bryce. "Looks like we have company. Two o'clock." Bryce had his arm wrapped around Zelda's waist.

"Damn. I was having fun. I guess we should leave before they spot us together. I'll call our driver." He kissed my cheek. "Meet you outside in ten. Tell Sam and Rosie bye."

I watched as he headed out the rear entrance. Back at our table, I explained the situation.

"But we were having such a good time," Rosie protested.

"Anytime you want to go dancing, Liz, give me a call." Sam handed me her business card. "How long are you in town?"

"I'm headed back to Charleston tomorrow. I'll be back on Sunday." I finished the last of my spritzer. "After that, I'll be around at least another couple of weeks. I'm working a case, and I have the piece of property I inherited to sort out."

Sam looked me directly in the eyes and placed her hand on top of mine. "If you need any help with your case, please feel free to contact me."

I was beginning to believe we could be friends. Maybe even good friends. "Thanks." I turned to Rosie. "It was great meeting you. Enjoy your long weekend in Cali."

I ducked out as Bryce and Zelda were headed toward the dance floor. I didn't know if Zelda spotted me.

Back at the house, I asked Brad, "Who do you think is better looking, Sam or Rosie?"

He replied without hesitation, "You."

I was encouraged by the fact that Duke didn't yip.

Chapter 14

Peanut's plan was coming together. As he whistled a tune, he unlocked the shed doors with the provided key. Then he tucked a thin nail in between the outside slats of the building. Later, it'd come in handy for picking the padlock. The shed had a few filthy denim overalls and dirty white t-shirts tossed in a corner. A pair would probably swallow him, but it'd do until he could find some proper clothes. He wasn't about to announce himself to the outside world with a Mission provided neon t-shirt.

Before dinner each evening, the Members and Newbies were given one hour of free time to do whatever. Exercise was encouraged, and Peanut used his hour to take long walks around the compound to plot the route from the sick bay to the gardening shed.

The sick bay had a back door surrounded by trash cans. If he could find a way to sneak out the door and duck behind the bins, he'd likely avoid the cameras. A tree-lined path would provide cover halfway to the shed. A cornfield would conceal him the rest of the way.

He'd wait for a cloudy night. He'd fake drinking the communal wine. After lights out, he'd stick his finger down his throat and throw up all over the floor. Then he'd moan and groan like he was dying. Once inside the sick bay, he'd find a way out that back door. If they put him in a damn hospital gown, that was OK. He'd change when he got to the shed, then hoist himself out the window and onto the roof. Using the rope, he'd lasso the tree and swing over to the other side. He'd walk until he found a road and hitch a ride back to town.

Peanut smiled as he imagined Rumor's reaction when she saw him.

Sure, it was risky. And he didn't know what would happen if he was caught. He hadn't heard of anyone who'd left after agreeing to stay, but this place was driving him insane. He couldn't take the god-like worship that people gave Apollo, or the crazy rules, much longer. As he lifted his head to the clear sky, he prayed for a cloudy night to come soon.

Chapter 15

Back in Charleston by early afternoon, I unpacked, creating a small pile of laundry. I hoped to finish packing for my return trip before my neighbors discovered I was home. While I placed a few pieces I wanted to take back with me on the bed, the hamster wheel spun in my head. Could a long-distance relationship work? Only time would tell.

On the plane, I'd read the magazine Tim had given me. The story about a surfing competition gone awry was well-written. After I'd paged through the rest of the publication, I'd drifted off to sleep. It felt strange to be home without Duke.

As I placed a few nightshirts on the bed, my thoughts were interrupted by the ring of the doorbell. I was surprised it took that long for the neighbors to realize I was here.

"Cassie, come in." She was the spry widow who lived a few doors down from me.

"I brought you some food." She handed me two Tupperware containers. "Pasta salad and brisket."

"Thank you." I kissed her cheek. "Would you like something to drink?"

Cassie followed me to the kitchen. "A cold water, please. I can't believe how hot it is. Summer's here in full force." She reached for a paper towel and wiped the perspiration off the back of her neck.

I placed the containers in the fridge and handed her a bottle of water.

She peered into the backyard. "Where's Duke?"

Before I could answer, the doorbell rang again. I opened the door and welcomed my neighbors Linda and Gwen inside. "Well, hello ladies. Come on in and join the party. Cassie's in the kitchen." The only female missing was my next-door neighbor, Maria. She was likely still at work. And of course, my best friend, Peg. She would have been the first to the door. My heart ached at the sight of her empty townhome across from mine.

"Welcome back. How was California?" Gwen tugged on her lime cardigan. How she could wear a sweater when it was nearly ninety degrees out was beyond me.

"Great," I grinned.

"We want the juicy details. Do tell." Linda cooed with a Canadian lilt.

"Chardonnay, Linda?" I ignored her comment.

Linda nodded.

Gwen added, "Make it two."

"I was about to explain to Cassie that Duke stayed behind with Brad. Looks like I'll be there a little longer than expected." I poured each of us a glass of wine.

Cassie put her hands on her hips. "Well, twist my arm. Pour me one too."

"I was just unpacking and repacking. C'mon back, I'll fill everyone in at once. Y'all can help me pick outfits." I led the way back to the bedroom. "I'm working on a case for Brad's company. I can't share a lot of details, but I'll likely be in Cali for a couple of weeks."

"Booger about the case, I want to hear what he's like in the sack." Linda plopped in one of the armchairs by the window.

"Linda," Gwen scolded, as she adjusted her spectacles.

Cassie chuckled and sat in the chair next to Linda's.

"Good, really good." I grinned.

"Look at that dreamy look on her face," Cassie teased. "But I am surprised you left your dog behind. You must trust Brad, a lot."

"Duke adores Brad and vice versa." I described how he'd made himself right at home.

Linda leaped out of her chair. "Oh, no, no, no." She picked up one of the nightshirts I'd set on the bed. "You're seriously not wearing this in front of that hot hunk of a man."

"Why not?" It was one of my favorites. A cartoon of a dog holding a coffee mug was on the front with a caption that read, "I'm Dog Tired."

"Don't you have anything lacy and sexy?" Linda asked.

I shrugged. My nightwear consisted of long T-shirts and comfy pajamas.

Linda's eyes twinkled. "We're going shopping tomorrow. Be ready at eleven."

"Can't. I'm meeting Jenny for lunch."

"Well then after lunch, Luv. No arguing."

Dang. How could I wiggle out of this? "You're hosting game night," I protested.

"Everything's just about ready," she replied.

I acquiesced. I knew Linda. "No" was not an option.

After an hour of gab and another glass of wine, the gang was all caught up, and I was almost packed. I dreaded tomorrow's shopping trip.

~ * ~

Since Peg's untimely death, her niece, Jenny, and I'd met most Fridays for lunch. The walk from my house to Southern Charm, my favorite tea shop, was steamy, but not unbearable. I was struck by the contrast between the coastal towns. Although I'd enjoyed the change in climate, the humidity seeped into my soul like an old friend. I inhaled the salty scent of the Atlantic Ocean. I was happy to be home.

Lou had ambushed me at the house this morning and demanded the details of my relationship with Brad. Lou and Brad had gone to high school together, and I happened to know Lou had a slight crush on Brad. We'd talked for an hour before I shooed him out so I could get ready for lunch. Jenny's boyfriend, Lawson, was joining us, and I was anxious to hear his initial findings on Brad's firm.

Southern Charm's owner, Ellie, greeted me at the door with a hug.

"Liz, I haven't seen you in a while. Where have you been?"

"California . . . a little cooler than here."

"That sounds divine. It's another hot one. We could definitely use some rain. Anybody joining you?"

"Two more."

She reached for a couple of menus. "I assume you want a table inside today. Where's Duke?"

"I left him behind with a friend in California." I followed her to a booth.

Jenny and Lawson walked in a few minutes later. I stood and waved them over to the table. Lawson wasn't tall, but he towered over Jenny's four-foot-nine-inch frame. He sported a well-trimmed goatee and glasses. His long dishwater blonde hair contrasted with Jenny's copper pixie. He looked a bit like Shaggy from Scooby-Doo. They made a cute couple.

After introductions, Ellie took our drink orders, and Jenny excused herself. "I'll let you guys have a few minutes. I need to buy a couple of gifts." She headed toward the selection of teas, teaware, various creations from local artisans, and other treasures.

Lawson didn't waste any time. "I'm still working on hacking MultiPoint's systems. So far, no luck. I need a couple more days, but I'm not ready to give up yet."

"OK." Brad would be encouraged by the news.

He handed me an envelope. "I did find out some interesting information about the prescriptions." Leaning forward, he said, "They were all prescribed by the same doctor, Dr. Robert Stanistreet. His address and information are in the envelope."

After I opened the envelope, I peered inside. Sure enough, Stanistreet was spelled exactly like Alice's last name. His office was in San Jose. This was an interesting twist. "Great work, Lawson, thanks."

Jenny returned with a couple of gift bags stuffed with colorful tissue. "Ellie makes it so easy." She placed the bags on the floor and slid into the booth next to Lawson. She picked up the menu. "What are y'all getting?"

"Probably the special," I replied. Today's feature was a Greek salad with grilled chicken and a cup of green gazpacho.

Ellie returned with our drinks. My mouth watered at the sight of my regular iced tea with a splash of sweet tea. When I'd tried to order the drink in California, the wait staff had looked at me like I was from some strange planet.

We ended up placing three orders for the special, and when Ellie left for the kitchen, I asked Jenny if Peg had ever mentioned Mission Apollo.

"Doesn't sound familiar." Her jaw dropped as I explained the set-up. "That's too weird. I need to do some research on that guy." Jenny was a research hound. She'd helped me out on Peg's investigation and aspired to be like Velma from Scooby-Doo. I didn't have the heart to correct her when she mistakenly called her childhood hero Thelma. One of these days, I'd break the news.

A few minutes later, Ellie arrived with our orders. While I consumed my cold soup and salad, I asked Lawson a deluge of questions about his background and his relationship with Jenny. He didn't flinch at any of them or hesitate to answer. Peg had asked me to look after Jenny in the letter she'd left behind for me, and I took the job seriously.

So far, Lawson was passing muster.

~ * ~

I longed for a nap. Linda had dragged me to two different lingerie shops and insisted I try on at least twenty pieces. A fortune later, I was now the proud owner of three silk and lace cami sets with matching robes. I snipped off the price tags and added the items to my suitcase.

My phone pinged with a text from Brad.

> Miss you. How are you doing?
> Great. It's good to see everyone. How's Duke?
> Good. We took a long walk on the beach this morning.
> I miss you guys.
> Tomorrow can't come soon enough.
> Ditto. I have a surprise for you.
> What?
> You'll find out tomorrow. ;)

After swapping my shorts for a pair of jeans, I walked to Linda's house with the bouquet of sunflowers I'd bought on the way home from our shopping excursion. I'd promised to help her set up for game night. The rest of the gang was due to arrive in half an hour.

Before Peg's death, I would've knocked on the door, opened it, and hollered a hello before entering. Now everyone had a security system. Linda disarmed the alarm and invited me in. "Hello, Luv. Did you tell the man about your new nighties?"

I handed her the bunch of blooms. "No. I want to surprise him." When we entered the dining room, I stopped and admired the décor. A bright yellow tablecloth covered the dining room table. Candles flickered, and an overflowing arrangement of citrus-colored flowers sat in the middle of the space. "Looks great, Linda. What can I do?"

"You can help me set out the nibbly bits." She motioned toward the kitchen. "Trays are in the fridge. Put the chips in the baskets on the counter. Let me put the poppers in the oven, and then I'll help you." She leaned over the kitchen sink and filled a vase with water. Snipping the ends of the stems, she placed the flowers in the vase. "Thanks for these." She set the vase on the kitchen table and then slid the tray of jalapeno peppers into the oven.

"You're welcome."

I pulled a veggie platter out of the fridge and started to fill the table with food. Cocktail shrimp in a bed of ice, a charcuterie board, a dish of pulled pork sliders, a plate piled high with fruit, a container filled with deviled eggs, and bowls of dips galore. Linda followed me and added serving spoons. She plugged in the warming tray for the poppers.

"You've outdone yourself. We'll never eat all of this food."

"I bet the boys will have no problem taking care of the rest." She chuckled.

'The boys' referred to Linda and Gwen's husbands, along with the two single men in our community.

She stepped back and observed the table. "Will you get the paper plates, napkins, and utensils? They're in a bag in the pantry."

I grabbed the bag and handed it to her, and she set out the additional items. "Trivia guy will be here at six. I thought we'd do individual instead of teams."

If Peg was around, we'd have two teams of three. I sighed as the doorbell rang. My next-door neighbor, Maria, had arrived. I excused myself, closed the door to the powder room, and dabbed at the tears streaming from my eyes. I missed Peg so much.

~ * ~

I left Linda's a little after eleven with a Tupperware container of deviled eggs she'd insisted I take for tomorrow's breakfast. In my other hand, I carried a bottle of wine, the prize for winning one of the rounds of trivia. We'd played three rounds. Gwen and Maria had won the other two.

The Uber driver would arrive at ten o'clock sharp tomorrow to take me to the airport. I'd be back in California by two in the afternoon, local time. I was a jumble of emotions. Although I'd enjoyed my time with my neighbors and being back home, I'd missed Brad and Duke. And I was anxious to resume the investigation. This time Brad would be picking me up when I landed. The butterflies in my stomach fluttered in anticipation of the reunion. I texted him and requested that he bring my dog to greet me.

Chapter 16

Apollo praised Cosmo's investigation efforts. He leaned forward. "I have a temporary assignment for you. I've made arrangements for someone else to cover your work for the next few days." He pointed at Cosmo, even though he was the only other person in the room. "You are to keep a close watch on Brad O'Connor's home." As he gripped the edge of the desk, he continued, "Be discreet and document every move the couple makes. I want to know when they eat and when they shit. I expect periodic call-ins and a written report at the end of each day. Got it?"

"Yes, sir." Cosmo saluted him on his way out.

~*~

Cosmo parked on the street two blocks down from Brad's house and walked toward the woods that bordered the property. Camouflaged by the foliage, he used high-powered binoculars to watch the home. A man let a dog out. Cosmo scanned the area to see if he could get closer without alerting the animal. If he went in the back and around the property to a clump of boulders, he might have a better view.

He climbed behind one of the boulders and surveyed the grounds. A woman with a vacuum cleaner entered the small house by the pool. When he zoomed in, he confirmed she wasn't who he was looking for. He breathed a sigh of relief when the man reappeared, held the back door open, and whistled for the dog. The floor-to-ceiling windows of the main structure made it easy to track him as entered the study and sat at a desk. Once he'd confirmed the man inside the office was Brad, he searched for Liz. No luck.

As he turned the lens toward the smaller structure, he watched as the woman raised the blinds and began to clean the glass. He'd a perfect view of what looked like some kind of board with words written all over it. He grabbed the camera out of his pack and snapped pictures, pausing when his legs started to cramp. Confident he'd gotten some good shots, he scurried down the beach to a line of trees where he could take a leak and scan the images.

After he relieved his bladder, Cosmo pulled up the pictures and reviewed them one by one. Holy crap. Looked like that PI, Liz was investigating something while she was in town. Why else would the words suspect and motive be written all over the board?

Cosmo couldn't wait to call his boss and tell him.

~ * ~

Around midnight, Peanut had walked down the hall of the sick bay to the bathroom. No one else was in sight. He strode right past the restroom and slipped out the back door. Peanut navigated the cornfield in the darkness while stalks slapped his body as he ran toward the toolshed.

He picked the lock within seconds. Once he'd slipped into the shed, he quickly changed into the overalls and t-shirt and pulled himself through the window. From the rooftop of the shed, he lassoed an overhead tree branch, swung across the fence, gathered up the rope, and then shimmied down the trunk of the sizable oak. He breathed a sigh of relief when he touched ground and tucked the evidence of his escape deep into a line of bushes.

Peanut did a little happy dance. He'd busted out. The moon was a sliver in a cloud-filled sky. As a bonus, a film of fog covered the night. The execution of his plan had been a breeze.

He hesitated for a moment before he headed what he thought was northwest. He'd no watch, no compass, and no flashlight. Hoping to make it to a road by dawn, he mouthed a silent prayer. So far, God seemed to be listening.

As he navigated his way through a dense forest of trees, he encountered multiple raccoons and opossums. Peanut wondered if he'd ever find a path out. He discovered the road as dawn broke. A couple of eighteen-wheelers passed him by before one finally stopped. He gratefully accepted the ride to the outskirts of Carmel. After he exited the truck, Peanut canvassed the shopping center where the panhandlers typically gathered. No one had seen Rumor in over a week. Not even her few trusted friends. He bummed money off a passerby and bought a prepackaged sandwich from a nearby market. As he hummed Ray Charles's "Hit the Road Jack," he searched for a place to settle for the night.

Once he found a hidden spot under a bridge by the Carmel River, Peanut had the best sleep he'd had in weeks. If he couldn't find Rumor tomorrow, he'd file a missing person report. He'd a lot to spill to the cops about Apollo's operations.

~ * ~

Apollo banged his fist on the table. "What do you mean you can't find him?" he roared at Cosmo and Atlas. Anxious to view Cosmo's photos, Apollo had summoned him to return to the compound immediately after their call. The pictures troubled him, and now Peanut was missing. Apollo paced the room and ran his fingers through his long wavy black hair. "Do any of the others know?"

Atlas hung his head. He was in charge of the sick bay. "Just us, boss. I informed Cosmo as soon as I discovered Peanut was missing."

Five minutes of silence passed as Apollo devised a plan. He pointed his finger at Atlas and shouted instructions. "You. Place a sign on one of the single rooms explaining that Peanut is quarantined. Inform the staff that you are taking care of him. Say we are worried he is highly contagious." His eyes narrowed as he wagged his finger. "You better not screw this up. Go."

"Yes sir." Atlas scooted out the door.

When he turned his attention to Cosmo, he growled, "Find something with Peanut's scent. Grab one of the dogs and see if you can track him down. Let's keep this quiet for now. If you find him, bring him straight to me. Any questions?"

"No sir."

Apollo shook his head. "I don't like this one bit, Cosmo. I sure as hell hope you find the fool."

An hour later, Cosmo returned to report that the bloodhound had followed Peanut's scent to the toolshed. Apollo grabbed the edge of the desk and leaned forward. "Where is he?" He roared.

"I don't know, boss," he replied. "The dog lost the trail."

"Take the dog to the other side of the fence. If he picks up the scent, report back immediately." As Cosmo headed for the door Apollo added. "And send Atlas back my way. Looks like we have a funeral to plan."

Chapter 17

I skipped down the private plane's steps and into Brad's arms. My dog jumped up and placed his paws on my hip. After a long lingering kiss from Brad, I loved on Duke. Brad opened the back of the Rover, and my dog hopped inside. The steward placed my suitcase in the backseat. Traveling private didn't suck. After I slipped into the passenger seat, I fastened my seat belt.

Brad turned on the ignition and drove toward the exit. "How was the flight?"

"Easy. Thanks for the lobster bisque." I licked my lips as I recalled the savory bowl of soup paired with a Greek salad. Post lunch, I'd taken a quick nap and then finished Sue Grafton's *S is for Silence*. I could identify with the main character, Kinsey. I was relaxed and ready for next week's challenges.

"How was Charleston?" Brad rolled the back windows down a third of the way for Duke.

"Wonderful. I enjoyed my visit." If only I could have the best of both worlds. As I picked at my cuticles, I wondered if this relationship would ever work with the two of us on opposite coasts. "Have you figured out what you want to do with Peg's townhome?" Peg had bequeathed her Charleston townhome to Brad.

"Not yet. Why do you ask?"

"Just curious."

Brad grinned, "Soooo . . . what's my surprise?"

I turned toward him and winked. "You'll find out later."

"The suspense is killing me."

"I do have some news for you on the case." I studied the lines of his face and added, "Good news and bad news."

"OK . . ." He drummed his fingers on the steering wheel.

"The good news is so far my computer expert has been unable to hack your systems."

Brad gave me a smug look. "I told you so."

"He hasn't given up yet. He wants a couple more days."

"And the bad news?"

I hesitated before I continued. "Alice's cousin is the doctor writing the false scripts."

"My assistant?" He chewed his lower lip while he digested the news. "That doesn't mean she has anything to do with this."

Duke poked his head between our seats and thumped his tail. "Maybe or maybe not. But I promise you I'm going to find out."

"That's why I hired you." He signaled a turn. "What time is your meeting with the real estate guy?"

I'd scheduled an appointment with the contact Brad had given me to discuss options for the property. As beautiful as it was, I couldn't picture myself holding on to it. "Four."

"I guess we have some time, then." He caressed my forearm.

My face grew warm as I replied, "Maybe I can show you your surprise."

~ * ~

I'd planned on modeling all three outfits. We didn't make it past the first one. Brad had appreciated Linda's efforts. He stayed behind to prep dinner while Duke and I drove to meet the agent. I'd taken the air horn just in case. After what had happened on my last visit, I wasn't taking any chances with potentially dangerous wildlife creatures.

Ken met us at the entrance to the property. His white hair contrasted with his dark spectacles. Dressed in jeans and a sports jacket, he looked professional. I unlocked the gate, and we drove our cars down the dirt road to the clearing. I snapped the leash on my dog and then motioned toward the picnic table. "I appreciate you meeting me here. Let's sit."

He took a seat and passed a file folder to me. "I pulled comparable properties and placed a few phone calls. How quickly do you want to sell?"

"I'm not in a rush."

"There's a real estate developer who's very interested. He'll pay top dollar. I've included his contact information in the file."

As I thumbed through the folder, I sighed. Would Peg want me to sell? She'd already accomplished her scheme to get Brad and me together. A bouquet of hummingbirds hovered over a mound of lavender wildflowers. Their ruby heads and emerald bodies sparkled in the late afternoon sunlight. The birds were Peg's favorite. I interpreted the sight as a sign that the time wasn't right. "I'll think about it." Closing the folder, I stood and tucked it under my arm. "Would you like to see the beach?"

"Sure."

Duke and I led the way down the path to the coast. "Do you mind holding this for me?" I handed the file back to him and pulled the air horn out of my pocket. As I diligently scanned the landscape for mountain lions, I kept my finger on the button ready to sound the horn. We made it to the shoreline without incident.

"This is stunning. I can see why you might be hesitant to sell."

"Damn. There's that creepy guy, Apollo." I pointed toward the entrance of a cave. "He's in almost the exact same spot as last time." I sounded the air horn to get his attention, as Duke emitted a symphony of barks.

"You get trespassers often?"

I tucked the device back in my pocket and watched as Apollo scurried off in the other direction. "Not that I know of. If I keep the land, I'll need better security."

"Good idea." Ken added, "You know . . . you could save yourself the hassle if you sold now. Would you like for me to reach out to the developer and find out if he wants to submit an offer? If we cut the work of listing it, I can give you a break on my fee."

"I'll think about it."

As I drove back to Brad's my mind whirled. Apollo kept showing up, and he wanted me to donate the land to his Mission. On one hand, a donation in memory of Peg seemed like a good idea. On the other hand, if I sold the property, I'd be able to retire from the PI business permanently. Did I want to quit a job I loved? And why on earth did she leave me the land to begin with?

*

"What do you think I should do?" I asked Brad while he tossed the salad.

"About Apollo or the property?"

"Both."

"You should give Sam a call tomorrow. See if she can charge Apollo with trespassing." He set the salad tongs on the counter and studied my face before he asked, "You're not thinking about donating it to the Mission are you?"

I set my elbows on the counter and placed my face in my hands. "I dunno. Would Peg want me to?"

"No way. Don't even consider it."

"You're right . . . but I can't figure out why she left it to me."

While Brad turned his attention back to dinner preparations, I opened the cabinet, took the plates out, and set them on the counter

After a few minutes of silence, he cleared his throat and said, "What do you think about moving to California?"

"Are you serious?" I took a step back.

"I missed you this weekend. It's hard having thousands of miles and a couple of time zones between us. Besides, Duke likes it here."

Stunned by the question, I grabbed a bottle of red from the wine fridge and poured myself a generous glass. "I don't think so." My voice caught, and I took a gulp of wine. "I have a job. I have a home. I have friends."

"C'mon, Liz. You don't really need the job. If you sell the property, you'll be set for life. You can take the plane back to visit your friends anytime."

I placed the wineglass on the counter and crossed my arms. "I like my job." My voice rose even though I was trying to control my reaction. "You want me to upend my life and move here just like that? No can do." While I glared at him, I added, "I'm not a California girl." Duke whined in the background.

Brad sighed, "It was only a question. I can live with the distance."

"Would *you* consider leaving everything and moving back to Charleston?" I asked indignantly.

He rubbed his chin. "I could work remote. Come back when needed." He nodded, "I might just do that."

Duke didn't yip.

Brad's comment threw me. I opened and closed my mouth twice before I found my voice. "I'm going to set the table." Without waiting for a response, I carted the plates and silverware to the patio. I needed some space. The sound of the ocean in the distance calmed my frazzled nerves. I thought about Brad's willingness to come to Charleston and sighed. The man continued to amaze me. He truly would be willing to do as he said. I silently thanked Peg for her note encouraging us to stay in touch after she passed.

Composed, I walked back inside and hugged Brad. "Thank you."

"For what?" he asked.

"For being you."

He responded with a kiss.

While the sun set, we ate our dinner of barbecued chicken, grilled asparagus, and salad by the pool and discussed the week ahead. We'd leave for San Jose on Wednesday morning. Tim had agreed to stay at Brad's and watch Duke while we were gone. The earlier tension had almost completely dissipated until I mentioned that I had a dinner date with Ted Oliver tomorrow. When I added that Duke was coming along to meet Ted's Russells, Brad protested. Dang. He'd become awfully attached to my dog.

~ * ~

Up early the next morning, I got ready for the day. As I powdered my nose, I heard a crash. I ran in the direction of the sound. Brad stood frozen in the kitchen staring at the tile. An empty saucepan teetered on the floor. "What happened?"

Speechless, he pointed at something on the other side of the kitchen island. When I peered around the corner, I discovered the source of his distress, a roach. I couldn't help the giggle that escaped from my lips. "Seriously? You're the CEO of a company, you run triathlons, you've overcome your fear of the water and of flying, and you're scared of a bug?"

Brad found his voice. "They're disgusting."

"Duke, get it." I pointed at the insect.

Brad backed up against the wall and watched as my dog chased the creature and then crunched it with his front paw. "Good boy." I rewarded him with a biscuit from the pantry before picking up the dead bug with a paper towel and tossing it in the trash.

Brad released the breath he'd been holding. "You know the fear of roaches is a real thing. I'm not the only person that hates them." He rubbed Duke's back. "Thanks, buddy."

"If you say so." I chuckled. "I guess I'll see you at the office." Duke and I had a full day of interviews ahead of us, and I had a few things to take care of before I left. After Brad kissed me goodbye, I placed a call to Sam and explained the situation with Apollo.

Sam asked, "Has he caused any damage to the property?"

"Not that I've noticed. I guess I can look a little closer."

"Unless he's caused some damage, I can't charge him with criminal trespassing. Do you have any no trespassing signs posted?"

I mentally added the item to my to-do list. "No. I'll do that this week."

"I can stop by his place and warn him. You might want to put some cameras up."

"I'll think about it. Thanks. I owe you a drink."

"I will definitely take you up on that offer." She paused, "Can I give you some advice?"

"Of course."

"I know you're working a case for Brad. You need to fill out a California Private Investigator's Reciprocity Form. You don't want to risk your findings not holding up in court. You can find it on our website, or I can drop one off."

I was liking Sam more and more. "Good point. I'll do it right away. Thank you."

"I'll call you after I visit Apollo. Then you can buy me that drink."

~ * ~

My first task when I arrived at the office with Duke was to pay a visit to Alice.

"Good morning. I wanted to introduce you to my dog, Duke."

"Well, hello." Alice patted him on the head.

"I Googled the name Stanistreet." Alice withdrew her hand and looked at me. I added, "I was curious when you told me everyone was related." She pursed her lips. "You have a relative in San Jose who's a doctor. Must be handy to have one in the family and so close by."

While she fidgeted with her earring, she replied, "Yes, my cousin, Bobby. In a family as big as ours, we have everything — a doctor, a dentist, a lawyer, even a beer distributor. My cousin, Mary Pat, is in charge of distribution for Labatt's in the US." Her voice warmed a little as she talked about each one.

"Do you see them often?"

"Other than reunions, not much. I meet up with Bobby occasionally for lunch on the weekend." She took her glasses off and wiped the lenses with a tissue.

So far not a single yip from my dog. Her phone rang. "I'd better get back to work. Have a good day."

I waved at Brad as we walked down the hall to Tim's office. After a few awkward sniffing moments, Duke and Tim's cat, Irish, became fast friends.

"Looks like Duke has a new best buddy," I commented.

Tim chuckled. "I swear Irish thinks he's a dog."

"By the way, I loved your story. You're very talented."

"Thanks."

"I'm serious. I'm an avid reader so I know good writing when I read it. Your story's excellent. You could easily turn that one into a full length-novel."

"I may have to think about that," Tim said, then added, "How's the investigation going?"

"Making progress." I sat down and logged into the computer. "I do have a question."

"Ask away."

"What kind of system access does Alice have?"

"She pretty much has the keys to the castle." He frowned. "You don't think she had anything to do with this, do you?"

"I haven't ruled her out as a possibility."

~ * ~

I spent most of the morning in a conference room interviewing employees in the customer service department. Zelda was the last on my list. She was the team lead for the call center.

"Sorry, I'm late. I had to take a quick cigarette break."

"I saw you smoking with Bryce. You two seem like good friends."

She pulled out a chair. "Just work colleagues. We've gotten to know each other a little over smoke breaks." Duke yipped.

"Nice dog." She patted him on the head. "What's his name?"

"Duke." I opened my notebook and prepared to take notes. "Tell me about your typical day." After she finished, I said, "I randomly pulled two calls from clients, and I'd like you to walk me through how you handled each of them."

She chuckled. "I hope I can remember."

"The first one was early February for a Mike Williams." I gave her the date and time of the call.

She squirmed in her chair. "Oh yes. I do recall that one. It was from his brother. He'd called to cancel the service. The client had died of a heart attack. His brother had a hard time controlling his emotions on the call." She walked me through how she'd dealt with the call, expressing empathy while taking care of canceling the account.

"The second one was from a Betty Miller on behalf of Joe Miller's account."

"Doesn't sound familiar."

My dog yipped.

I reminded her of the date and the time.

"I don't remember that one at all."

He yipped again.

Zelda looked his way. "What's wrong with your dog?"

"I think he needs to go out. That should do it, Zelda. Thank you for taking the time to answer my questions."

I had a break before my next interview, so I paid a visit to the receptionist. From my previous corporate experience, I'd learned the receptionist typically knew all the office dirt, especially if they'd been with the company for a while. Cindy had been with MultiPoint since the start.

"Hi, Cindy."

"Howdy, Liz," she replied with a Texas twang. Her Maltipoo slept curled in a dog bed on top of the desk. "How's everything going?"

"Good. I just finished my session with Zelda." Duke sat next to my feet and looked up as I stroked her dog's back. I leaned forward and whispered, "So, what's the scoop on Zelda and Bryce?"

She rolled her eyes. "Oh, they act all professional in the office, but everyone knows they're dating." She pulled her long dishwater blonde hair into a ponytail holder and fashioned it into a makeshift bun.

"You've worked here a long time. You must know all the office secrets."

"I've been here since the beginning. I know a few." She winked.

"Like what?"

"Like the VP of Operations hates the VP of Marketing. She constantly drones on about him to me. And Lisa's pregnant." She placed her hand over her mouth. "I probably shouldn't have told you that. Please don't tell anyone. Lisa wanted to wait to share the news after her first trimester."

"I won't tell a soul," I replied as I tried to remember who Lisa was. "So, what's Brad like as CEO?"

"Great. Couldn't ask for better. Brad is incredibly generous, and he remembers everyone's name. We're like a family."

I wondered if she layered on the praise because I was his friend, but Duke didn't yip. "What do you think about Alice?"

She shook her head. "Not a fan. I guess she does a good job for Brad, but she walks around like she has a corncob stuck up her you-know-what."

I laughed and silently agreed.

"By the way, I'm so envious," Cindy said.

"Why?"

"You get to share an office with Tim. I have a huge crush on him. It's too bad Fifi and Irish don't get along."

A visitor approached the reception desk, and she dismissed me. "Thanks for stopping by Liz. Come visit anytime."

My afternoon interviews consisted of a handful of employees from the sales and marketing group. No yips, but I did learn more about SecureLife which would come in handy on my date with Ted this evening.

Chapter 18

When the blare of the air horn sounded, Apollo darted out of sight. Once he'd circled back around, he peered into the clearing where the two cars were parked. He clenched his fists when he spotted the real estate logo and phone number plastered on one of the cars. Then he pulled out his phone and snapped a picture. Was she thinking about selling? He ran his fingers through his hair. Time to ramp up his efforts and delay tactics.

He stepped away and placed a call to Cosmo.

"Boss, I was just about to call you and give you my report. Liz must have left town for a bit, but now she's back. She and that guy pulled up to the house earlier and unloaded a big suitcase. Looks like she might be in town for a while."

"I want you back at the compound," Apollo whispered. "There's been a change in plans."

Apollo shook his head. As if he didn't have enough problems. That damn woman kept showing up on his sacred ground. If she sold out to some developer, his whole world could come crashing down.

Sequestered back in his office, Apollo furiously jotted down ideas to deter a potential sale. Wife number four rapped on the door. "Sir, you have a visitor."

"Don't waste words woman. Who is it?" he bellowed.

"A female cop. Says she needs to see you."

He hoped the cop was here to report she'd found Peanut dead on the side of the road. His Mission Apollo badge would connect him to the compound. After he'd flipped the legal pad over, he said, "Send her in."

Sam strode in and offered her hand. Apollo wiped his sweaty palms on his pants before he accepted.

"How can I help you?" he asked.

"I understand you've paid a few visits to a piece of property on the coast." She rattled off the address.

"May have. I don't remember." He cleared his throat. "Is there a problem?"

Sam placed her hands on her hips. "It's private property. You're trespassing."

His body tensed as if he might pounce if further provoked.

"I'm here to warn you," she continued. "Stay off or you'll be charged with trespassing." Sam turned and exited, nearly colliding with Cosmo. He started to say something about the dog finding the scent, but the look on Apollo's face stopped him. He'd wait until the cop was out of earshot before he reported the news.

Minutes later, Atlas arrived, and Apollo ushered them into the conference room and shut the door. The silence was deafening as Apollo gathered his thoughts. Cosmo and Atlas stood rigid and awaited direction.

They both jumped when Apollo bellowed "sit" and nearly tripped over each other before taking their places. Apollo commanded from the head of the conference table. "Peanut has accomplished the unthinkable. He managed to escape and return to the streets. This is unacceptable, and we must not let anyone else here know." His electric blue eyes bore into each of their faces. "Understood?"

"Yes, sir." They replied in unison.

"Atlas, wait until dark, then fetch one of the wooden coffins. Fill it with enough stones to equate Peanut's approximate weight and nail it shut. Tomorrow, we'll announce that he's passed. Then you'll make a show of disinfecting the room he was in. You can put the coffin in the chapel. Any questions?"

Atlas shook his head.

"Cosmo, draft an announcement for my review. And plan the service. I'll break the news at breakfast, and we'll have the funeral tomorrow afternoon. You can recruit a couple of the Members to dig the grave after breakfast."

"You need me to draft the eulogy?" Cosmo asked.

"No, I'll do that myself."

Both men pushed their chairs from the table and prepared to stand.

"Stay put. I'm not done." He looked directly at Atlas. "I have a way for you to redeem yourself."

Atlas leaned forward, eager to get back in his good graces.

Apollo proceeded to give Atlas the information he'd gathered on Liz along with instructions to run her off the road asap. "I don't want you to kill her. Just scare her. Although if you manage to kill her, I won't cry." He brushed his hands together. "You're both dismissed." While he leaned back in his chair, he laced his fingers behind his head and looked toward the ceiling. Perhaps if he could frighten her a bit and get her off balance, she'd reconsider donating the land.

Everything he'd built was at stake.

Chapter 19

My date with Ted and his dogs was at a rooftop bar off Ocean Avenue. Luckily, Brad wasn't home when I left with Duke. I didn't think he'd appreciate the extra spritz of Amazing Grace I'd layered on. Or the peasant top with a plunging neckline and the matching flouncy skirt. The flat sandals made it easy to navigate the downtown streets of Carmel.

When I arrived, I spotted Ted's dogs lapping from a plastic water bowl at a corner table. They yapped as Duke and I approached. I noticed Ted didn't bother to stand or pull out a chair for me. At least my dog had manners. He sat and offered Ted his paw.

"You look lovely." He looked me up and down, his eyes settling on my chest.

"Thank you. How was your day?" I took a seat and studied the happy hour menu. Ted motioned for the waiter.

"The usual, investor calls, presentations, meeting after meeting. If you don't mind, I'd like to order a bottle of wine to share. It's one of my favorites, a red blend."

"OK."

He turned to the waiter. "A bottle of the Conundrum red." After the server left, he turned back toward me and said, "It's from a California winery. I know the owners. I think you'll like it."

His dogs were finally yapped out, and Duke was curled by my chair. I started to relax. "Tell me about your work."

He droned on about his company and the identity theft protection business. I was beginning to feel like an expert.

The waiter returned with a bottle of wine and two glasses. Ted tasted and nodded his acceptance. The server poured each of us a full glass.

After I inhaled the rich, red liquid, I took a sip. "Delicious." The flavor of berries and chocolate with a hint of smoke was divine.

"I'm glad you like it."

I steered the conversation back to the earlier subject. "Do you have a lot of competition?" I asked.

"We have several competitors, but we're the best," he boasted. "One of them's close by, MultiPoint. They don't have near the experience and expertise we do." Duke raised his head and yipped which set the Russells into another barking frenzy.

"Quiet boys," Ted bellowed and rewarded them with a treat when they calmed down.

The waiter returned to take our food orders. After he stepped away, I asked, "How do you manage to stay ahead of the competition?"

He winked. "Oh, I have my ways." A few moments passed, and he switched the subject, "Tell me about your divorce."

After fifteen minutes of sharing mutual divorce woes, the waiter arrived with our food. I'd ordered the sanddabs, a local fish. Ted had ordered a steak. I noticed he didn't share any with his pups. While we finished our meals, we discussed our favorite movies and books. Our tastes were on the opposite ends of the spectrum. He preferred biographies and horror films to my mysteries and romantic comedies. The waiter cleared our plates, and I stood to say goodbye.

"Please let me walk you to your car."

Well, maybe the man had some manners after all. "That's not necessary."

"I insist."

Ted paid the bill, and we strolled toward the Mustang. As we walked, he pointed out his favorite places along the way. The Russells attempted to keep up with Duke's stride.

"Nice 'Stang. Rental?" he asked.

"Yeah. Cost me, but I thought it'd be fun to drive a convertible along the coast." Duke yipped.

"I'd like to see you again. Maybe this weekend?" He walked over, cupped my face, and brushed his lips against mine.

"Sure," I replied, concocting excuses in my head as my dog let out another yip. "Call or text me."

Back at the house, Brad and I sat outside. He grilled me about my dinner with Ted and winced when I mentioned I might go on another date with him. I didn't like Ted's 'I have my ways' comment. Might also need to pay a visit to his ex.

We both scrolled through our phones as we listened to Otis Redding croon "Sittin' on the Dock of the Bay."

After I opened the email from Lawson titled, 'I give up,' I turned to Brad. "Good news. You're unhackable. Just got the word from the computer expert."

"Best news of the day." He whistled for Duke. "Let's go celebrate."

~ * ~

While I sipped my first cup of hot tea for the day in the guesthouse office, I added a couple of new suspects to the list. Alice,

Zelda, and Bryce. I'd no concrete reason to add Bryce, but something about the guy bugged me. I caught up on my notes and updated my index cards. Before I left with Duke for the next round of interviews, I sent a quick text to Ted and thanked him for last night's dinner.

This morning I would meet with Tim's staff. I hoped to glean some additional information about the auditor, Bryce. Tim's lead accountant was happy to oblige. She gushed on about how cute Bryce was and filled me in on the details of his divorce. The split had been nasty and expensive. When I asked how she knew all the history, she said her sister was friends with his ex. She dismissed my questions about Bryce and Zelda's relationship. "I don't think it's anything serious. They're mostly smoke buddies." Duke didn't yip once during the interview.

My phone buzzed as I was taking him outside for a pee break. "Hi, Ted."

"You bitch." He screamed into the phone. "Is this some scheme to get at SecureLife?"

"I don't know what you're talking about."

"Don't go all dumb blonde on me. I ran the plates, and I ran a background check on you. I know your connection to Brad."

I silently cursed myself for giving him my real name. My mind churned as I fumbled for a believable story. Instead, I deflected, "You run background checks on all your dates?"

"I learned from my divorce." He growled. "You stay way the hell away from me and my company. You'll pay if you don't." He hung up.

Well, I guess that was one way to get out of a second date. I shot off a quick text to Brad.

> Busted. Ted knows I'm friends with you.

Seconds later, my phone buzzed. This time it was Sam.

"I paid a visit to Apollo. He was clearly agitated when I told him he needed to stay away from your property."

"Thanks, Sam. I owe you that drink."

The tone of her voice shifted to one of excitement. "Sounds great. I'm off this Friday. Maybe we can squeeze in a little dancing, too."

"Awesome."

"I'll see who's playing and text you on Thursday." She hesitated then added, "By the way, about Apollo . . . be careful. He seemed like a guy on edge. If he shows up again, call me."

We returned to the conference room and wrapped up the interviews with the employees from Tim's department. Duke's lie detector hadn't gone off once. My phone pinged with a text from Brad.

> Join me for lunch in my office.
> Sure. I just finished. Be there in ten.
> I want to hear about your conversation with Ted.

Back in Brad's office, I took my place at the table. My dog was in luck. Today's boxed lunch was a French-dip sandwich. He'd love polishing off any leftover beef broth. After I'd unwrapped the meat-laden roll, I asked, "How was your morning?"

"Productive." He sat and opened his box. I wrinkled my nose at the fishy smell. He'd obviously chosen the tuna salad croissant sandwich.

Neither Duke nor I could stand tuna salad.

"Tell me about the call from Ted."

"He called me a bitch. Told me to stay away. Don't think I'll see him anytime soon," I joked. "Guess I'll have to find another way to dig for information." I bit into my sandwich and licked the oozing horseradish off my lips.

Brad grimaced. "That SOB. How dare he threaten you." He reached for his phone.

"Please," I pleaded. "Leave it. If he's the one behind this, we want him rattled."

A few moments of silence passed as I watched Brad wrestle with the urge to call Ted. He nodded then said, "What about Mitch? He never struck me as a loyal employee. He might be willing to spill if there's any dirt."

"Good idea." I slipped Duke a stray piece of roast beef. "I have his address. Maybe I can stop by his place on my way back home tonight."

Brad offered my dog a bite of his sandwich. Duke took one sniff and walked away.

"Guess he doesn't like tuna." Brad placed the morsel on a napkin. "If I remember right, Mitch was one of those seven-to-four guys. Early in, early out. You might want to confirm that with Tim." He grinned. "Don't be too long. Tomorrow, we head to San Jose."

Post lunch, I conducted the afternoon interviews with the Operations group, and then called it a day. Satisfied I'd sampled a pretty good portion of the MultiPoint population, I packed up my computer, index cards, and files. I thanked Tim in advance for watching my dog while were in San Jose.

Then I headed to Mitch's place.

~ * ~

Once parked in front of Mitch's house in Pacific Grove, I watched for a few minutes and then stepped out of the car with Duke. I wished the Mustang was a little more nondescript. Clipboard in hand, I rang the doorbell. When the doorway opened, I immediately recognized Mitch from the photo . . . curly sandy brown hair, tortoiseshell glasses framed amber eyes. He'd either changed to shorts or wore shorts to work. His legs were toned as if he were a regular jogger.

"Hello, I'm Liz." I stuck out my hand.

He reluctantly shook it. "Nice dog."

"This is Duke. MultiPoint Protection's hired me to help improve employee retention rates. Since you left the company, I wondered if you might have a few minutes to answer some questions about your experience there." I handed him my card.

He shrugged. "Sure. Come on in."

I loved how the whole Monterey area was dog friendly. Mitch didn't think twice about inviting us both in. I took a seat at his kitchen table. The bay window had a view of the deck in the backyard. "Nice house."

"Thanks."

"I promise not to take much of your time. Tell me about your experience in the Customer Service Department and why you decided to leave."

Mitch filled me in and commented that it wasn't his gig. When presented with the opportunity, he'd left to work for SecureLife. The substantial pay increase had influenced his decision.

"What's it like at the new company?" I asked.

Mitch perked up. "Awesome. It's great working with numbers and analyzing the competition. Right up my alley."

"How's the culture compared to MultiPoint?" I asked.

He shrugged. "I dunno." Glancing at the clock on the microwave, he asked, "Are we almost done? I'm supposed to meet a friend for happy hour."

"That's all I have. If you think of anything that might be helpful, please call me."

I nudged my doge awake, and we followed Mitch to the front door.

As I drove down the street, I reflected on the conversation. How did analyzing the competition connect with stolen identities? Maybe if your job was to bury the competition?

I wished I felt closer to finding the culprit. Perhaps San Jose would provide some answers.

I signaled a left and turned toward Highway One. "Life is a Highway" by Rascal Flatts played on the radio. I tapped my fingers to the tune. The darkly tinted windows of a Black Toyota Camry caught my attention in the rearview mirror. I was surprised there wasn't more traffic on the two-lane road. Next thing I knew, the vehicle sped alongside me. When I slowed to allow the driver to pass, he pulled directly in front of me.

I slammed on the brakes and swerved to avoid a collision. The Mustang ran straight into the guardrail.

"Damn California drivers," I screamed, pounding my fist on the dashboard as the Camry sped away. Duke whined. "You OK, boy?" I ran my hands across his head and body. He didn't seem any worse for the wear. Just shaken up. Like me. We were lucky. I stepped outside to inspect the damage to the vehicle. The right front bumper was dented, but the car was drivable. As I climbed back into the driver's seat, I remembered Ted's words. Had this been deliberate? Had Ted been that angry?

As I pulled back on to the road, I wondered how I'd explain this one to Brad.

*

While I stared out the living room windows and watched the waves lap the shore, I took deep breaths and attempted to settle my nerves.

"What happened to the Mustang?" Brad asked as he closed the front door.

I plopped into a chair, sighed, and explained that I'd been run off the road and into the guardrail on the side of the highway.

"Are you OK?"

"Duke was with me. We're both a little shook up, but we're not hurt." I sheepishly added, "I'm sorry about your car."

He laced his fingers behind his neck and paced the length of the room. "I don't care about the car." He halted and faced me. "Do you think it was deliberate?"

"Yes," I reluctantly replied.

"Any idea who?"

"I didn't see the driver. The windows were tinted. I'm pretty positive only one person was in the car. It was a black Toyota Camry."

"You get a plate number?"

"I wish." I sighed.

"Any idea who could've done it?"

"Not sure. But I do wonder about Ted."

While I filled him in on the full extent of my conversation with Ted, Brad became increasingly agitated. He reached for his phone. I stood and put my hand over the screen.

"Not yet. Somebody is rattled, which means I'm getting close. Please don't call Ted."

He set the phone down and gritted his teeth. "Whoever it was could've killed you both."

"I don't think that was the intent. It was only meant to scare me."

Brad took a few deep breaths before he replied, "I need a drink. Glass of wine?"

"I think I need something stronger."

He grinned for the first time since walking through the door. "I know just the trick."

Brad returned and handed me a coral-colored drink in a martini glass.

"What is this?"

"My own concoction. I've been told it tastes like something you'd experience on a tropical island."

I took a sip. "Tasty. This will definitely take the edge off."

He tossed back half his glass of scotch and kissed my forehead. "You've had a bad day," he said before he sat in the chair opposite me. "And you scared me. I couldn't stand it if something happened to you or Duke." Downing the rest of his drink, he added, "At least we'll be in San Jose for the next two days. Away from all this."

I breathed a sigh of relief.

He set his drink down and smiled. "Take your shoes off. I'll give you another one of my famous foot massages."

I didn't need a second invitation. I flipped off my sandals and propped my feet on the table. Brad had given me a foot massage when he was in Charleston for Peg's funeral. His skills were world-class.

Chapter 20

Peanut had searched the riverbank and the shopping centers for five hours yesterday. Once more his efforts to find Rumor, or anyone who'd seen her in the last week, were fruitless. His heart sank. Apollo had claimed you would be returned to where you came from if you decided not to stay. Something wasn't right, and he decided that he was going to the cops today. As he scratched the center of his widow's peak, he tried to remember the name of the nice female cop who had never hassled the homeless. She often grocery shopped in the center where he typically panhandled, and she always brought him a bottle of water. Some boy's name. He ran through the alphabet and stopped at S. That's it. "Sam." When he got to the station, he'd ask for her.

After he'd bathed in the river and cleaned himself up the best he could, he headed downtown.

~ * ~

The front desk clerk peered into Sam's office. "A guy asked for you. Says he wants to file a missing person's report. You got time?"

"Not really, but send him back." Sam recognized the homeless man as soon as he walked through the door. "Well hello, Peanut."

"Hiya, Ms. Sam. Thanks for seeing me. I got me a bit of a problem."

"Have a seat. What's going on?"

As Peanut explained the disappearance of Rumor, Sam filled out the missing person form for him. She wasn't sure if he could write, and she didn't want to embarrass him. Peanut provided physical characteristics and listed Rumor's usual hang-out spots and habits. Sam remembered occasionally seeing the woman on the streets.

While he disclosed more about his experiences at Mission Apollo and his search for Rumor, Sam's hackles rose. Something suspect was happening on at that compound. She reached over the desk and patted Peanut's hand. "I'm going to find her for you. Don't you worry."

As Sam watched him walk out of her office, she hoped that was a promise she'd be able to keep.

Chapter 21

After an easy drive to San Jose, we pulled up to the Hayes Hotel in a nondescript black Honda Accord I'd insisted on renting for my surveillance work. Brad had booked us into a suite earlier.

When I entered the palatial set of rooms with sweeping views, I gasped. "Wow. Not too shabby." The king-sized bed was piled high with pillows. I peered into the bathroom and blushed as I pictured us together in the spacious marble hot tub.

Although the change of scenery was welcome, I'd had a hard time leaving my dog behind after yesterday's debacle. He seemed fine, but I imagined that, like me, his body was sore from the jolting stop. Tim assured me he'd keep a close eye on him. He and Irish were staying at Brad's house so that Duke didn't have to be introduced to another new environment.

Back in the main area, I set my computer bag next to a sprawling desk. I fished out the surveillance kit I'd remembered to pack when I'd returned to Charleston. As much as I'd like to take advantage of the hot tub now, I needed to get started.

"You're not leaving?" Brad frowned.

"You want me to solve this case, don't you?"

"Sure. Just didn't think you'd head out right away."

"How about we plan for a date in the hot tub later? My aching muscles will need it." I rubbed my sore neck.

"You got it. I have some work to do, too. What time will you be back?"

"Sevenish?"

"Maybe we can order dinner in the room." He pulled me close and kissed me. "Good luck."

~ * ~

I pulled the Honda into a space in front of the offices of Dr. Robert Stanistreet and watched patients entering and departing. His website claimed he specialized in pain management. The building looked like a doc-in-a-box. I walked in hunched, with my hand on my back and a grimace on my face. "I'm in a lot of pain," I explained to the receptionist.

"You have an appointment?"

"No."

She pulled up the calendar on her computer. "I could get you in tomorrow at four."

"Please," I pleaded. "I'll pay cash."

"Name?"

She wrote my name on a slip of paper. "Have a seat. I'll see if I can work you in."

Thirty minutes later, I was in front of Dr. Stanistreet. He was at least five years younger than Alice. Slightly overweight, he sported a military-style haircut. Wire-framed glasses perched on a hawk nose. Eye problems must run in the family. He wore a heavy gold necklace and a couple of diamond rings. After he'd asked me a handful of questions, he scribbled out a script for pain meds.

While I paid my five-hundred-dollar tab, I envied his hourly rate.

I tucked the script into my tote and drove toward the Galaxy Apartment Complex. No one answered at apartment 201 or any of the surrounding apartments. When I stopped by the leasing office, I was disappointed to find a sign on the door claiming they were out to lunch. Strike one.

I picked up a turkey club sandwich from a nearby deli and proceeded to the next complex on the list. After I parked in a vacant reserved spot close to apartment 107, I watched while I ate my sandwich. Fifteen minutes of zero activity passed before someone in a white truck honked at me. She rolled down her window.

"Excuse me. You're in my spot."

"I'm so sorry. I was waiting on my friend. He lives in 107."

"You'll likely have a long wait. I never see anyone go in and out of that place."

I pulled out of her space, parked in the next available empty spot, and then hopped out of the car. She was unloading grocery bags from the passenger's seat. "Any idea where I might find him?"

"You might check in with the apartment manager." She paused in thought. "Occasionally I see a guy pick up mail from the 107 mail slot."

"When does the mail typically arrive?"

"In the afternoons. Around two."

"You need any help?" I motioned to the grocery bags.

"Nah, I got this. Thanks though."

I walked to the manager's office. The woman on duty was a young redhead. Couldn't be older than twenty. She didn't know anything about the tenant in 107. When I asked her about leasing a place for myself, she fumbled with the forms and the details for securing an apartment. I mentally prepared to stake out the mailboxes tomorrow.

While I drove to the Paradise apartment complex, I tested a theory in my head. Dr. Stanistreet writes the scripts. They are filled online and sent to various apartments leased to stolen identities. Some stooge comes along, picks up the prescriptions, and then sells them on the black market. I imagined it was a lucrative business.

Before I climbed the stairs to apartment 323, I placed a call to my new computer buddy, Lawson. "Any chance you can find the next delivery dates on the prescription information I gave you?"

"Piece of cake," he replied.

When I reached the third floor, I paused as my phone pinged with a text. Lawson was quick. He already had the dates. I was in luck. Two of the addresses were receiving a delivery tomorrow. I rapped on the door of 323. No answer. I knocked on the door of 322 and waited for someone to respond. No one did.

I had better success with 321. After a minute, a young man opened the door. The smell of weed was overpowering. "Um, I'm looking for my friend, Will. He lives in 323. Do you know when he'll be home?"

"Lady. Nobody lives there. I ain't never seen no one." He slammed the door in my face. My theory that nobody really lived there looked promising.

The manager at this complex was more helpful than the woman at the first complex. I pretended to be interested in leasing. She showed me the various floor plans and handed me an application. "What time does the mail usually arrive?" I asked, adding, "I run a mail-order business. The time of day and predictability are important to me."

"Around noon. There's also a FedEx office down the street if you need something expedited." She leaned forward and pushed for the sale. "If you put down a deposit of five hundred dollars today, I can hold an apartment for you. I'd urge you to do so, we're filling up fast."

"Thanks. I'll think about it."

I had no luck at the last apartment complex on the list, but I was satisfied with the progress I'd made today. The two solid leads were also the locations of tomorrow's deliveries. On the way back to the hotel, I placed a call to Gunner. I wanted to test my theory on him. He agreed that my hunch was promising. Good. I was finally making progress on the case, and I couldn't wait to update Brad.

Back in the suite, I nearly tripped over the side-by-side massage tables set up in the living area. Brad handed me a robe. "I thought you could use this after yesterday."

I tilted my head from left to right and attempted to ease the knots in my neck. "Great idea. Where are the masseuses?"

"In the bathroom washing up." Brad slipped off his robe and climbed under the sheet face down. A male and female masseuse walked our way, the male cracking his knuckles. His hands were huge. I headed toward the bathroom to change.

As I slipped under the sheets on the table next to Brad, he asked, "Any progress on the investigation?"

"Hmm. I'll tell you later." I sighed as the male masseuse spread lavender-scented hot oil on my back and used those giant hands to work on the kinks. An hour later, my body felt like a limp noodle. Brad signed the check while I filled the whirlpool bath with hot water.

In between kisses, we filled each other in on our days. Breaking the golden rule of not getting involved with a client didn't seem like such a bad idea after all.

~ * ~

After Brad and I worked out in the fitness center the next morning, I took a quick shower, then wolfed down a pastry and added a banana to make it a balanced meal. Since I had some time to kill before the mail deliveries would arrive, I planned to circle back to see if I'd have better luck with the last two apartments on yesterday's list. On the way, I placed a call to Tim.

"How's Duke?"

"Great. I just dried him off from a swim. Guess I didn't dry him off well enough," he chuckled.

Relieved he felt OK to take a swim, I waited for Tim to continue the story.

"I'm trying to coax Irish out from under the sofa. As soon as I let Duke in, he shook water all over him. My cat hates to get wet."

"Other than that, are they getting along OK?"

"Thick as thieves," he replied.

I grinned as I hung up the phone. Before we'd parted ways, Brad revealed that he'd arranged for a private dinner at a local winery this evening. He was officially my new favorite travel agent.

I looked forward to later.

The manager's office was open at the first complex on yesterday's list. A woman who appeared to be in her forties chatted about the apartments and the tenants. She leaned forward and said, "If you want to get a good feel for the atmosphere here, talk to Penny. She's in 111." She had the raspy voice of a smoker. "Penny knows everyone."

I thanked her for the information and headed to 111. A sixty-ish woman, whom I assumed was Penny, answered the door immediately. Her Pomeranian barked incessantly. "Don't mind Lucy." She put her foot in front of the dog to prevent her from escaping. "I'm Penny. How can I help you?"

I introduced myself and explained that the apartment manager had directed me her way. Behind her, I saw a stack of mystery books on the coffee table. When I shared that I was a private investigator, she immediately welcomed me inside.

"I'm looking for information on the person who lives in 201."

"Oh my. Yes, I can tell you about that man."

We settled into her living area where her pet promptly jumped on my lap.

"Lucy!" Penny chided.

"She's fine. I love dogs," I replied as I massaged Lucy's ears.

Penny explained that while she never saw the man go inside 201, she did see him stop by the mailboxes on a regular basis. "I can't stand tattoos." She shook her head. "This man has a pair of dice tattooed on his neck. Can you imagine? That had to be painful."

"I can't. Never wanted one myself."

She stood. "Where are my manners? Can I get you anything to drink?"

"No. Thank you. I can't stay long. What else can you tell me about him?"

"Well," she raised her eyebrows and cocked her head. "Lucy can't stand him. Barks like crazy every time she sees him. Don't you, girl?"

Lucy wagged her tail.

Penny patted her on the head before she took her seat. "I've always thought that dogs had a good sense of people. That man is bad news."

After my visit with Penny, I headed directly to the Paradise apartments. There was no time to visit the other apartment where I'd struck out yesterday. I parked in a spot with a view of the mailboxes and fetched my camera from my tote. Zooming in, I located the mailbox for 323 and waited.

The postal worker showed up shortly before noon. Thirty minutes later, a gray Ford pickup parked in a visitor's spot, and a man in a black hoodie emerged from the driver's side. He was about six feet tall. His jeans were torn, and he wore black high-top tennis shoes. The hoodie made it difficult to see his face. All I could make out was a goatee and a mustache. He appeared to be of Hispanic descent. I focused the lens as he turned the key to the mailbox for 323 and snapped several pictures. The box he extracted had the logo for RXFast printed on the side. As he drove off, I jotted down the license plate number on the back of the vehicle on my notepad.

I waited for fifteen minutes and then slipped the fingerprint kit out of my tote and lifted prints off the mailbox slot. I planned to ask Sam if she could run the prints through the national criminal database.

Time to move on to the next stakeout.

I stopped in a convenience store to relieve my bladder and bought a bag of corn chips and a bottle of water. The snack should tide me over until dinner. Stationed in place by one-thirty, I munched on the chips and waited. An elderly woman with pink hair walked to the mailboxes with her Chihuahua. She pulled an armful of mail out of her box as the postal worker drove up. Looked like she hadn't checked her mail in a week. This time, I'd positioned myself to have a better view of faces.

Minutes after the mail truck drove off, a gray Ford pickup pulled into the lot and parked. The same hooded guy got out. When the wind blew the hood off his head, I zoomed in with the camera lens and snapped several pictures. He had a six-inch scar that ran down his left cheek and a distinctive tattoo. A couple of dice covered half his neck. Couldn't be a coincidence. Had to be the same guy Penny had described. He turned the key in the mail slot for 107 and retrieved a box with the RXFast logo. Once he was back inside his truck, I turned on the ignition and prepared to follow him. This was getting interesting.

Trailing behind, I tailed him to a bank, where he made some kind of transaction via the drive-through. His last destination was a trailer park on the east side of the city. Definitely my lucky day. I had his prints, his photo, the location of his personal bank, and his address. If my luck continued, I'd be back at the hotel by five.

Heavy San Jose traffic had other ideas.

My phone rang as I inched along in traffic. "Hi, Sam. I'm so glad you called. I have a favor to ask."

"What do you need?"

I shared the information I'd gathered and asked if she could run the prints and plates on 'dice guy.' "I completely understand if you can't. I wouldn't want you to get in any trouble."

"Since I'm now officially Sherriff Sam, I don't think that'll be a problem."

"Congratulations, boss lady. I look forward to celebrating with you tomorrow. Did you pick a place?"

"Thanks. That's one of the things I called about." The new sheriff rattled off a name and address. "Can you text it to me?" I asked. "I'm driving."

"Of course."

"Was the promotion your other news?" The speedometer inched up to seven miles per hour.

"Actually, no." She filled me in on her conversation with Peanut. "You buy those no trespassing signs, yet?"

"Not yet."

"Get them as soon as you can. I'll help you post them." She paused, and then continued, "I'm not getting a good vibe about Apollo."

"Yeah. I'm with you." I promised to buy the signs soon. "When I get back to the hotel, I'll send you a couple of photos of 'dice guy' along with the plate numbers."

By the time I made it out of the traffic snarl to the hotel, I had just enough time to send an email to Sam and freshen up before dinner.

~ * ~

In case the winery was cold, I'd bought a cream pashmina shawl in the gift shop on my way up to our room. Brad was already dressed to go. He looked handsome in a navy sports coat and starched white shirt. I changed into a coral halter dress and added strappy gold sandals with a bow in the back. I spritzed my favorite perfume on my wrists and neck.

"You look lovely." He nuzzled my neck, "And you smell good."

"Thank you." Somehow, he could still make me blush. On the thirty-minute Uber ride, I updated him on my progress and the discovery of 'dice guy.' It felt like a break-through. I was ready to celebrate over several glasses of wine.

When we arrived at the winery on the outskirts of town, I soaked in the view. A sprawling gray house with a wrap-around porch was surrounded by acres of grapevines. Rolling hills were covered in wildflowers. Horses munched on grass in a fenced-in area. We were greeted by the owners and the resident mastiff. As I patted the large pup's head, I missed Duke even more. I couldn't wait to see that boy tomorrow. The couple who owned the winery ushered us to the back patio where a bottle of cabernet and a charcuterie board waited. A fire pit crackled nearby, but there was enough chill in the air that I pulled the shawl around my shoulders.

As I loaded a sampling of cheeses and meats onto my plate, I said, "Oh, I forgot to tell you earlier. Sam got promoted to sheriff." The French bread was warm and looked homemade. The server poured a sample of a deep ruby liquid into Brad's glass.

He sipped the wine and then nodded his approval. As the waiter filled both our glasses, Brad said, "Great news about Sam. Seems like you two are getting along."

I savored the grape flavors layered with chocolate and vanilla and began to relax. "Yeah, she's alright."

Our starter of a variety of cheeses, meats, olives, and thin crackers was followed by a garden-fresh salad with a light vinaigrette dressing. While we ate, the sun descended behind the mountains turning the sky a rainbow of colors. When our entree of beef tenderloin topped with a wine reduction sauce arrived, I practically drooled. "Maybe I could be a California girl after all."

Brad placed his hand on top of mine and gazed into my eyes. "You mean that?"

"Maybe." I wondered if Duke was around if he would've yipped. Although I had started to open my heart to Brad, could I ever fully trust another man again? And could I actually leave my Southern roots? I wasn't so sure about the truth in my answer.

Chapter 22

Apollo stood proudly at the head of the table. "I thought the funeral went well and the eulogy was brilliant."

"Yeah, boss. You had 'em all in tears," Cosmo commented.

Apollo grinned with satisfaction. As he released a deep breath, he leaned forward. "It's time to get back to the business at hand. We still need to find Peanut." He pointed to Cosmo. "Get one of your minions to take over your duties for the day. I want you to comb Carmel for Peanut. If you find him, sedate him and bring him to the property." He smirked. " Then we can have a second funeral for him."

"Yes, sir."

Apollo continued, "Atlas, good job running that woman off the road."

Atlas gave Cosmo a smug look.

"But you're not done."

Atlas's grin faded.

"Someone else will take care of your job for the next few days. I want you to tail Liz Adams." Apollo slid the folder over with her details. "Be discreet, but make her life as difficult as you can. Throw nails down by her parked car. Slip a laxative into her drink. Get creative."

Atlas nodded.

Apollo addressed both of them. "I expect periodic call-ins and a written report at the end of each day. Got it?"

"Yes, sir," they responded in unison.

He slid an envelope overflowing with cash to each of them. "Use whatever you need to grease the wheels. Your assignments are mission-critical. You're both dismissed." He paused for effect before bellowing, "Cosmo, don't come back until you've found Peanut."

After they left, he opened the secret door disguised as a bookcase and climbed down the stairs to the underground tunnels that connected his living quarters, the office, warehouse, chapel, and front gate. Time to check on the progress of the latest shipment. As he navigated his way through the narrow wooden passageway, he silently congratulated himself for the genius of the design. The tunnels allowed for packages to be dropped off and picked up at the front gate undetected. They also provided an easy way to transport the sedatives for the communal wine.

He opened the door to the warehouse and observed two of the Disciples and three of his wives at work. In a darker corner of the room, wife number two hung cannabis plants to dry. Special jars for the curing process lined the shelves. The two Disciples sorted the latest shipments into labeled bins. They didn't bother with expiration dates. His other wives printed shipping labels and prepared the packages. Ambien, Xanax, Ritalin, Oxy . . . he strode through the space and greeted each of the workers. Satisfied the operation was running smoothly, he picked up a fully cured jar of cannabis and headed back to his quarters for a quick hit.

~ * ~

Cosmo decided to start his search in downtown Monterey. The city harbored a larger homeless population than Carmel. If he was Peanut, that's where he'd go, not back to where he'd been picked up. Determined to make his boss proud, he canvassed the streets and showed Peanut's picture to shop owners and panhandlers. Seven hours later, his feet were swollen and throbbing, and he had zero leads. Apollo phoned twice asking for an update. Cosmo dreaded the next call. He called it a night and checked into a motel. Tomorrow, he'd start in Carmel bright and early.

Chapter 23

We were on the road by seven a.m. Brad was anxious to get back to the office. Tim was at the house awaiting our arrival. Duke howled "I love you" as soon as we walked in the door. I scratched his back and rubbed his ears while Brad filled Tim in on our trip and my findings.

"Thanks for watching him," I said.

"He was easy, and Irish will miss him," Tim replied. "They slept curled up next to each other last night."

Duke bounded over to Brad and demanded attention. His tail swished in the air. "Hey, boy. I missed you too." Brad opened the pantry, grabbed a rawhide, and handed it to him. While Duke munched on his treat, Irish playfully pawed at the bone.

"So, what's next?" Tim asked.

"I'm going to get the computer expert to try to pull bank statements for this guy I saw picking up mail at the two apartments."

"And I'm getting serious about next weekend's triathlon." Brad patted his stomach.

"You guys need me to watch Duke?"

I looked at Brad. The half Ironman was in San Diego.

"Come cheer me on, Liz," he pleaded.

"Alright." Then, feeling guilty, I patted my dog. "Sorry, boy."

"It's only Friday night. We'll be back on Saturday," Brad said.

"Yeah, maybe I'll have the case solved by then." I sighed.

Once Tim and Brad left for the office, I called Lawson. He agreed to the additional work and hoped to have an update by the end of the weekend. Banks were tough to hack. He'd made no promises. I unpacked and then headed for the guesthouse. In the quiet and comfort of the office, I reviewed the whiteboard and added the details I'd gathered on 'dice-guy' and Dr. Stanistreet. There were two people I hadn't explored yet, Ted's ex and Chandler Price, the triathlete. He lived in a condo not too far from where I was due to meet Sam this evening. Maybe I'd stop by his place first.

I fired up my computer, logged into my background check software, and entered each name on the suspect list. Alice was squeaky clean. I wished that I had her credit score. Ted had a lot of debt, and so did Bryce. Bryce's credit score was lousy. Nothing stood out on Mitch and Chandler's reports. Sally had an unpaid parking ticket. I switched gears and searched social media. Chandler was a selfie pro. He'd posted pictures of various competitions, including a few photos with his finishing times. Alice had a lot of friends. Most of them with the last name of Stanistreet. As expected, Sally posted lots of pictures of her kids.

I pushed back from the desk and stood to stretch my legs. As I stared at the list of suspects, I scratched my head. I was almost two weeks into the case. Even though I felt I was getting closer, the truth was I had no clear evidence that any of the people on the list were the culprit.

Ted had the clearest motive, wanting to bury his competition and revive his company. I put a number one by his name. Perhaps

Mitch collaborated with him. I drew an arrow between Mitch and Ted. Alice was connected through her cousin, but I had no idea what her motive might be. She seemed to adore her boss. I put a number two by her name and added 'Motive?' According to Tim's accountant and the credit report, Bryce was hit pretty hard financially by the divorce. Money was a powerful motive. I put a number three by his name. I prayed Sam and Lawson would uncover some information that would break the case.

My phone rang, and I was surprised to see a call from Lawson. "What's up?" I didn't expect to hear from him so soon.

"I took the day off so I could get you some answers."

"I hope that doesn't get you into any trouble."

"Nah, it's cool. I found out some interesting info."

I heard a rustling of papers in the background. "The bank account you had me check is registered to a Luis Lopez. So far, I don't have details on him. Still working on hacking into the account to retrieve his statements."

"Great work, Lawson. Thanks for getting me the name so quickly."

"You're important to Jenny, so this is important to me."

The young man was impressive. After I ended the call, I turned to Duke. "You hungry?" He couldn't race to the door fast enough.

~ * ~

On my way to visit Chandler before meeting Sam, I stopped at a hardware store and wiped out their supply of no trespassing signs. Since the Mustang was still in the shop, I'd driven the Mercedes. I tossed the signs in the trunk and backed out of the space. As soon as I reached the exit, the tire pressure light flashed. I pulled over to the side and climbed out of the car to take a look. Sure enough, both rear tires were low. When I peered closer, I spotted the nails. Damn.

I called Brad.

"What's up?"

While I explained my dilemma, I hoped he had roadside assistance. Although I could change a tire, no way could I do two. Even if I wanted to. Plus, I was wearing my favorite pair of white jeans. They'd be ruined. I gave Brad the address. He promised help would be on its way soon and asked that I text him as soon as they were done. Yikes, I wasn't having the best of luck with his cars.

Road service arrived within minutes.

As I watched the technician change the tires, I wondered how I got the flats. The roads here were pristine. The nails must've shown up after I parked. I couldn't imagine any other scenario. The spot next to me had been empty. I remembered backing up from the parking space and then pulling forward. Had I run over something with the two rear tires? Was it a fluke? *Probably not.*

Thirty minutes later, I texted Brad to tell him the car was fixed. Then I was on my way to visit with Chandler.

From my earlier research, I'd learned he was an active member of the Democratic party. I rapped on the door of his condo and hoped he'd buy my survey ruse. A tall, chiseled guy with wet, tousled hair answered the door. He looked like he just stepped out of the shower. "Good afternoon, I'm with the local precinct of the Democratic party. I wonder if you'd have time for a quick survey? It won't take more than ten minutes."

"You are?" He extended his hand.

"Liz."

"And I'm Chandler. Sure, why not? Come in. You want a beer?"

"Oh, I don't think we're allowed to drink on the job." I batted my eyelashes.

"One beer won't hurt. Have a seat."

"OK, twist my arm." I settled into the far end of a u-shaped tweed couch. A couple of issues of *Triathlete* magazine were on the coffee table. I thumbed through a copy. He returned with two cans of a local IPA.

I set the magazine back on the table and gushed. "Are you a triathlete?"

He handed me the beer and sat a few feet away from me. "I am."

"Thank you." I popped the top and asked, "How long have you been competing?"

"About five years. Training for the San Diego half Ironman right now." He looked me up and down. "You ever thought about it? I could train you."

"Hmm, maybe." While I sipped my beer, I sauntered to a trophy case nestled in the corner. "You have a lot of wins. What do you get when you win?"

"Just bragging rights and points toward All World Athlete status. I missed the cut last year thanks to this guy named Brad." He spat his name out like bad medicine.

"Who's Brad?"

"My nemesis. Weren't you going to ask me some survey questions?"

I smiled as I pivoted back toward him. "Oh yeah, I almost forgot."

After I took my seat on the couch, I asked a few innocuous questions about voting preferences and issues of importance I'd prepared in advance. Then I hurriedly exited before the conversation turned personal.

~ * ~

I parked the car down the street from the bar where I was meeting Sam. Chandler was competitive, but I agreed with Brad. He'd take the direct approach if he wanted to eliminate him from the competition. Distracting him by targeting his company didn't guarantee any results.

As I entered the Lion's Den, Sam stood and waved at me from a booth close to the stage where Jukebox Jams would play later. "Cute top," I commented as I slid into the seat across from her. She wore a sleeveless leopard blouse that showcased her toned arms. "Sorry, I'm late. I had a couple of flats earlier."

"Oh, no. What happened?"

I filled her in on the details. "Based on my luck, Brad may forever ban me from using his cars." I shook my head in disbelief. "I hope you weren't waiting too long."

"Actually I was running late myself. We had another tourist lose their cell phone."

The waitress appeared. "What can I getcha, ladies?" She tapped her pen on the pad while she waited for a response.

"You wanna share a pitcher of sangria?" Sam asked.

"Sounds good."

After she jotted down the order, our server asked, "You ladies eating or just drinking tonight?"

"I'll take a menu," I said. Sam nodded, "Make that two."

"Before I forget." I dug in my purse for an envelope. "Here are the fingerprints of that guy I need info on. And I have a name, Luis Lopez." I slid the envelope across the table.

"Ahead of you. I ran the plates. Guy's got a record. Calls himself '*Dice Man*.'" She handed me a folder. "Here's a little light reading for later. Previous addresses. Relatives. Just about everything you'd want to know."

"That's great. You deserve more than just a drink." As much as I wanted to read it right now, I slipped the folder into my tote.

"You can buy dinner." She winked.

The server returned with a pitcher of wine packed with slices of citrus. She placed it on the table and handed each of us a menu. "Let me know when you're ready to order."

I poured the purple liquid infused with fruit into mugs and raised my glass. "Congratulations, Sherriff Sam."

She smiled, "It does have a nice ring to it, doesn't it?"

"Sure does." We clinked glasses. "By the way, I bought the no trespassing signs today."

"Great. I can help you post them. How about Sunday morning?"

"That works." I wasn't in a big rush. "You heard any more from that homeless guy?"

"Peanut? Not anything since he stopped by my office the other day."

While I perused the menu, I asked, "What's good here?"

"The roasted mushroom and spinach pizza is to die for. I usually add grilled chicken to it. You want to split one?"

"Sure."

Sam motioned for the waitress. After we placed our order, she asked, "How long are you in town for?"

"At least through next weekend. I promised Brad I'd cheer him on next Saturday in the triathlon in San Diego." I stirred my drink with a straw.

"Soooo . . . what's the deal with you and Brad?"

I hesitated. Was she asking as a friend, or was she fishing because she was still interested?

She added, "I mean, obviously he's smitten with you. I've never seen any man look at a woman the way he looks at you."

I deflected, "You ever been married?"

She fiddled with the salt and pepper shakers. "Yeah, once. He was my high school sweetheart. We got married by the JP the day after graduation. Lasted almost four years."

"What happened?"

"He cheated on me. We were young. In hindsight, I should have seen it coming. All the signs were there."

I shared with her what happened with my ex. "So, you can see why I'm not ready to give my heart away. Plus, Brad lives in California, and I live in South Carolina. How is that going to work?"

She shrugged. "If it's right, you'll figure it out." She refilled our glasses. "You know I'm a lot more observant because of what happened with my ex. Helped make me a better cop."

The waitress arrived with our pizza. I placed a piece on my plate and let it cool for a minute before taking a bite. The crust was cracker-thin, and the tomato sauce appeared to be crafted from fresh tomatoes. Roasted mushrooms were perched on perfectly wilted spinach. On top of the mushrooms were bite-size pieces of grilled chicken drizzled with melted mozzarella. As I raised a slice to my lips, I considered Sam's comment. Before I took a bite, I said, "You know, not only are you a badass sheriff, you're also pretty wise."

"And don't forget a helluva dancer." She picked up a slice of pizza and then sighed, "Eat and drink up, so we can work this off on the dance floor later."

Chapter 24

Atlas slid into the booth behind the cop and Liz. He didn't think either of them would recognize him, but he wasn't taking any chances. After he ordered a burger and a Coke from the server, he listened to the girls' conversation. When he overheard Peanut's name, he nearly choked on his water. Apollo would not be happy Peanut talked to the cop. He pulled a pen out of his front pocket and began jotting notes onto a napkin. He didn't want to forget a single word of this conversation.

Earlier, he'd followed Liz from Brad's home to the hardware store. Once she'd parked her car and entered the building, Atlas had dropped a handful of nails behind her rear tires. He'd pulled into a nearby parking spot and waited for her to return. The incident didn't seem to faze her. Soon she was back on the road. As he followed her, he'd scratched his head trying to think of other ways to distract her. He hoped their conversation would give him some new ideas.

When the band started to play, Atlas paid his check and slipped out. He could barely hear his own breath over the beat of the music.

He wouldn't be picking up any more tidbits tonight. Once outside, he immediately phoned Apollo.

"He what?" Apollo screeched.

Atlas repeated, "Peanut went to see the cop that visited the other day. I heard her say it, boss."

"What did the idiot tell her?" He ran his fingers through his curls as he walked back and forth.

"I don't know. She didn't say anything about why he went to see her."

"Get back here pronto. I want a full report."

~ * ~

Apollo hung up the phone before Atlas could reply and rang Cosmo.

"Hi, boss."

"You found him yet?" Apollo asked in an agitated tone.

"No, sir. I promise I'm looking everywhere. If he's here I'll find him."

"Oh, he's there alright," Apollo told Cosmo about Atlas's report. "Amp up your efforts. It's imperative that you find him. Do you understand?"

"Yes, sir."

Apollo stood and paced his office. He didn't like how this was playing out. First, the woman who owned the property cramped his visits to the sacred ground. To top it off, she met with a real estate agent. Was she truly thinking about selling? Now this problem with Peanut and his visit with the cop. That would surely cause the police to poke around in his business. His entire carefully planned world might come tumbling down.

He needed to regain control of this narrative soon.

~ * ~

When Atlas returned to the compound to give his full report, Apollo could barely control his anger. Beads of perspiration appeared along his hairline. His right foot tapped on the floor. He didn't like that Liz was in cahoots with the cop, who according to Atlas, was now the sheriff. Swift action was needed if he wanted to avoid implementing the Mission Abort plan. He sucked in a deep breath and looked up at Atlas. "Good work. There will be a change in duties. I'll have someone else on the tail if needed."

Atlas's pulse quickened.

As he leaned forward, Apollo shook a finger in the air. "I want you at the local gun range practicing. Use the long-range rifle. You remember how to shoot?"

"Yes, sir." Atlas had earned his sharpshooter badge when he was in the Army.

"Good. Start first thing tomorrow following breakfast. Report back after practice." He snatched Atlas's notes. "You're dismissed."

Chapter 25

Brad set a steaming mug of coffee on the bedside table along with two aspirin and a bottle of water. "Morning, Sunshine."

Sam and I had Ubered our separate ways last night around one a.m. When I'd entered the bedroom, Brad had been softly snoring with Duke curled at his feet. I yawned, "What time is it?"

"Nine o'clock."

I sat up. "Ugh. I can't believe I slept so late."

"How was your night on the town with our new sheriff?" He looked down at Duke. "I'm allowed to ask that, right?"

We were still navigating how his lie-detecting skills fit into our relationship. "Of course. It was fun. The band was great." The group had started with a cover of Cyndi Lauper's, "Girls Just Want to Have Fun." Sam and I had danced until they quit sometime after midnight. I chased down the aspirin with a gulp of water and added, "I took an Uber home. The Mercedes is downtown."

"We can pick it up later. What do you have going on today?"

"I want to start in the guesthouse. I need to update my notes." I also wanted to digest the folder from Sam. "Later, I might do a little surveillance on Alice," I added.

I sipped on my coffee as I contemplated Alice's possible involvement. So far no motive. However, I hadn't ruled her out as a suspect.

"How about I whip up some breakfast and bring it out to you?" Duke's ears perked up at the word breakfast. "Maybe I can help you."

"Sounds good." A fresh set of eyes wasn't a bad idea.

While I waited for Brad, I read through 'Dice Man's' file. After he graduated from high school, he joined the Army. He was dishonorably discharged for selling drugs on base. Currently unemployed and collecting unemployment, he'd been arrested for stealing vehicles twice. The vehicle thefts were part of a larger ring that sold the parts on the black market. His girlfriend had a restraining order on him.

I set aside the list of relatives and acquaintances for later, logged into my computer, and opened my email. Amidst mostly junk was an early morning note from Lawson. Attached was a copy of Luis Lopez's latest bank statement. I shot off a quick reply.

> Thanks for this. Great work!

In minutes, my inbox pinged with a response.

> You're welcome. Took me a bit. It helped that it was a smaller regional outfit.

I studied the documents. For an unemployed guy, he had a lot of cash in his account. I was reminded of Gunner's advice . . . follow the money.

Brad entered the room balancing a plate in each hand. Over breakfast tacos with eggs, cheese, bacon, and avocado, I asked, "What can you tell me about Alice?"

Brad looked down at Duke, who was begging for a bite.

"Do I need to put him outside?"

"No." Brad slipped him a sliver of bacon. "She's worked for me for over six years."

I interrupted, "I'm talking about the stuff that's not in her personnel file. Hobbies. Love life. What she likes. What ticks her off."

"She's never been married. No boyfriends that I know of." He wiped a stray piece of egg off his lips with a napkin. "She adores her nieces and nephews. Does what she can to help fund their educations."

Interesting. Perhaps money was her motive. "That'd cost a pretty penny . . . she has a lot of nieces and nephews. She also lives in a pricey part of town." I'd seen the records. Brad paid her well, but not that well.

He shrugged, "I think she's done OK with her investments over the years."

I jotted down notes. "What about hobbies?"

"She plays bridge. Likes to read and travel." He placed his plate on the floor for Duke to polish off the crumbs. "She has a female friend she travels with." While he rubbed his chin, a few moments passed before he remembered her name. "Harriett. She lives in the same neighborhood as Alice. They like to take those high-end cruises."

I picked up the eraser, wiped out the question mark by her name, and wrote in money.

"You don't really think she's behind the security breach, do you?"

"Not ruling it out." I turned back toward him. "Keep going. What pushes her buttons?"

"She's a bit of a perfectionist. She doesn't like change. I drive her crazy sometimes when I come up with something new or when my schedule gets upended."

I imagined any assistant would have trouble keeping up with Brad's calendar.

"She gives me the silent treatment when she's mad. Doesn't last long. She has a major sweet tooth. I bring her a chocolate bar, and we're all good. I keep a stash in my desk." He chuckled. As he studied the list, he asked, "Why do you have Bryce on there?"

"Nothing specific. Just a hunch. What can you tell me about him?"

"He's not the friendliest guy, but he does a decent job. Very professional. I sit in on the meetings he has with Tim each quarter. I've been impressed." He shrugged. "I guess he could potentially get his hands on sensitive information, but why?"

I raised my fingers and rubbed them together. "Money. He had an expensive divorce." I paused. "By the way, I met with Chandler yesterday."

He raised his eyebrows.

After I filled him in on the meeting, I added, "He called you his nemesis, but I agree with you. He'd figure out a different way to side-line you from the competition. Interfering with the business would be too much trouble."

"I'm betting Ted's responsible. He's desperate to boost SecureLife's position in the marketplace."

"True, but why hasn't he leaked your security problems to the press?"

"I don't know. I wouldn't put it past Ted to have some grand scheme to destroy me when the time is right. The company will be releasing second-quarter earnings soon. It'd be a way to put the media attention somewhere else." He placed his elbows on his knees and rested his chin in his hands.

"Are we getting any closer to cracking this case?" he asked.

Duke nudged his elbow with his nose.

"I have some new leads to follow up on from Sam and the computer expert." I chewed on my lower lip. "Might be time to pay Ted's ex a visit." Brad sighed. I placed my hand on his shoulder and added, "I promise . . . I'm going to figure this out."

He raised his head. "I sure hope so and soon. There are a lot of employees and clients depending on me. This company is my family."

~ * ~

The pressure from my earlier conversation with Brad intensified my efforts to solve the case. I placed a phone call to Bryce. Surprisingly, he agreed to meet with me. Brad dropped me off to pick up the Mercedes, and I drove to Bryce's apartment.

Bryce opened the door moments after I knocked. "Thanks for agreeing to meet with me on a Saturday," I said.

"Come in." He motioned me inside. "I didn't feel comfortable talking to you in the office. MultiPoint's my client too. I do have a few ideas about improving their processes. I don't think Tim would like it if I hadn't shared my ideas with him first, so this is between us, OK?"

"Of course."

As I followed him, I noticed an expensive leather couch and a big-screen TV. "Nice set-up," I commented.

He grimaced, "My ex got most of the furniture. I had to buy all new stuff." He gestured toward a tan leather recliner. "Have a seat."

"That sucks."

"Yeah, she had the better lawyer."

I pulled my notebook out of my tote and clicked my pen. "OK. Let's get started. Tell me your ideas."

He had a few interesting ones, including analyzing the call center calls for any trends. Bryce leaned forward and asked, " What have you learned so far?'

"What do you mean?"

Turning his palms upward, he said, "What are your recommendations? You know, just between us."

I set my pen down. "I have some thoughts around tightening the security of the data."

He leaned back against the couch and narrowed his eyes. "Like what?"

"It wouldn't be fair to share with you before I share with Brad and Tim." Time to change the subject. "I saw you out dancing with Zelda the other night," I winked.

He stood almost toppling over the coffee table. "You must be mistaken." He pivoted toward the front door and grabbed a pack of cigarettes from the end table. "I need a smoke. Are we done?"

"Yes, that should do it. Thanks so much for your time."

"No problem." His tone didn't match the words.

As I drove back through town, the sign for the Carmel Bakery caught my eye. Ted had told me it was one of the oldest buildings in the city. I recalled Brad's earlier comment about Alice's sweet tooth and an idea percolated. After I parked the car, I phoned Alice. When I asked if we could meet to plan a belated surprise birthday party for Brad, she agreed and invited me to stop by her home in half an hour. I jotted down the directions.

The beige and red building of the bakery beckoned. As I peered through the glass window, my eyes feasted on the treats. Cannoli, cookies, brownies, pretzels, and caramel-covered apples were piled on white cake stands of varying sizes. My mouth watered. I entered the store, stepped into the long line, and observed what each person ordered. When it was my turn, I ordered two each of the pistachio and chocolate-chip cannoli. I couldn't get to Alice's fast enough.

Alice lived two blocks from the beach. When I found Bluebird House, I wondered how she could afford the place. The shingled blue New England-style home was surrounded by camellias, hydrangeas, and roses. The welcome mat had *Please Wipe Your Feet* in big black letters. A straw wreath, covered with pink shells of varying sizes, hung on the wooden door. I rang the bell and waited for Alice to answer.

"Hello, Liz. Please come in."

I made a show of wiping my feet on the mat and held up the bag of goodies. "I brought treats."

"Lovely. Let's sit in the kitchen. I'll put on a pot of tea."

As I passed oil landscapes framed in gold scattered along the entryway hall, I commented, "You have some beautiful paintings."

"Thank you. I've been amassing a collection of upstate New York paintings. I'm starting to run out of room."

When we entered the kitchen, the faint aroma of fresh paint hung in the air. The speckled gold granite countertops glistened, and the polished stainless-steel appliances looked brand new. Alice filled an electric teakettle with water. She pulled a couple of plates and teacups from the cream-colored cabinets and placed them on the center island.

"I love your kitchen."

"I just remodeled. It was a mess for months. I'm pleased with the results." She set out a selection of herbal teas, a bowl of sugar, and a jar of honey. "Help yourself."

I selected a pistachio cannoli and chamomile tea. As I balanced the plate and steaming cup, I took a seat at the kitchen table. I motioned toward a brochure for a cruise to the Greek Isles. "Planning a trip?"

"Yes. My friend and I love cruises. We're traveling in early October."

I picked up the pamphlet and thumbed through the pages. "Looks luxurious."

Alice sliced her fork into a chocolate-chip cannoli. "Shall we get started?"

In between bites of pastry, we planned the birthday party for Brad. "These are fantastic." I closed my eyes and savored the flavors. The crunch and saltiness of the pistachios perfectly balanced the sweet cream. Alice dabbed at the bits of cream on her lips with a napkin. "Pure heaven," she said before standing and adding another cannoli to her plate.

Once we'd polished off the sweets and finished the party plans, Alice asked, "How's the project coming along?"

"Great. I hope to present the final report with recommendations next week."

"Are you proposing any major changes?" She licked the last bits of cream off her fork.

"Mostly around data security."

She straightened in her chair. "Why? Brad's always boasted that's our greatest strength."

"Everything can be improved."

"That's silly. If it isn't broken, why fix it?" She stood and gathered the empty plates. I took her gesture as my cue that it was time to leave.

As I drove away, I remembered that Ted's ex's home was a couple of blocks from Alice's place. A wooden sign engraved with the word "Namaste" hung from the door of a sprawling two-story white stucco structure. I parked in front, searched my brain, and tried to invent a tale for my surprise visit. A tall woman dressed in a yoga top and pants walked down the driveway and rapped on my window. I pressed the button and rolled the glass down.

"Are you the bimbo who's picking up the spare set of clubs Ted left behind?"

"Um, no. I'm a bit lost. I'm trying to find Bluebird House."

"Oh, I'm so sorry." She looked horrified. "Ever since my divorce from that man, I haven't been myself. Please excuse my manners. I should've left the clubs on the curb." She looked at the ground while she readjusted her long black ponytail. "I just wanted to see what his latest girlfriend looks like."

"I understand. I'm divorced myself."

"Then you know how awful it can be." She shook her head.

"Must've been a tough one," I added, hoping she would elaborate.

"It was. Not only did he cheat on me multiple times, he also blamed me for everything that went wrong with that damn company. Like I had anything to do with it." She shrugged.

"Wow."

"Thank goodness we settled for the value of the stock at the time. It's gone in the tank ever since." She glanced at her watch. "The bimbo better show up soon. My yoga class starts in fifteen minutes."

"Can you direct me to Bluebird house?" I asked.

"Sure." She rattled off directions. "That would be Alice's place. She's the assistant to my ex's major competitor." She leaned in closer. "Between you and me, Ted is ruthless when it comes to competition. He plays dirty. I'd let Alice know her boss should watch his back."

Hmmm. That was an interesting tidbit. I thanked her for the directions and pulled away

As I drove back to Brad's, I mentally reviewed the list of suspects, Both Bryce and Alice had access to data, although I'd found no evidence either of them had accessed the files of the victims. I made a mental note to recheck the records. Maybe I'd missed something.

Ted remained my top suspect. Questionable character and desperate, a bad combination.

~ * ~

Brad and Duke were swimming in the pool when I returned. "Join us?" Brad asked.

"Give me a bit. I need to do a little work first."

He sighed. "OK. Fill me in later?"

"Of course."

"Great. I'm grilling tonight."

"Sounds wonderful." I hoped protein and veggies would counterbalance my earlier sweets splurge.

As I settled into the office space, I reviewed Luis's bank statement. All of the deposits were in cash and under ten grand. The deposits were frequent. Automatic debits were set up to pay the trailer park, car insurance, and electricity. There were also weekly Federal Express charges, but nothing else. He must pay all his other expenses with cash. I wondered if he was shipping the drugs somewhere. Maybe Lawson could find out. I composed an email with the details. Within a minute, my computer pinged with a response. *On it.*

Next, I turned my attention back to the computer records Tim had provided. I tapped my fingers on the desktop to an imaginary tune. I needed to approach this from a different angle. I'd looked at who'd accessed the records. What if I looked at the log-in activity around the dates of the thefts? Bryce's computer was supplied by the company he worked for, and he had a connection that allowed him to access MultiPoint's shared folders. As I reviewed the activity on the same dates, I discovered nothing out of the ordinary. Another dead end. I switched my focus to Alice. She'd opened an Excel file stored in a project folder on the dates in question. The file was titled *Executive Report*. I scratched my head and wondered what was in the report. I didn't remember the document coming up during the process review sessions. I made a note to ask Brad.

After I stretched my arms to the ceiling, I powered down the computer. Time for a break.

I found Brad in the kitchen with a towel wrapped around his waist. A wet Duke wagged his tail while Brad prepped the chicken. "Can I help?"

"You can pour us each a glass of wine." He nodded toward the wine fridge. "There's a nice chardonnay that should go well with the grilled chicken."

"This one?" I held up the bottle.

"Yep."

I uncorked the wine and poured two glasses.

"So, what's the latest?" He placed the prepped chicken to the side and washed his hands.

"First, I have a question." I smelled the wine before sipping. Peach, lemon, and vanilla notes tickled my nose. "What's the *Executive Report*?"

Brad dumped a bag of baby spinach into a colander and rinsed the leaves. "It's a report that summarizes the monthly highlights for each department. Alice prepares it for Tim and me." He set out a cutting board and trimmed the asparagus. "She also pulls together some stats on the customer tickets that were logged for the month."

"How does she get the data?"

"Each VP sends it to her, and she consolidates the information."

"What about the information for the tickets?" I didn't see any evidence she'd logged into the ticketing system when I'd reviewed her log-in activity.

He shrugged, "No idea. I don't get that far into the weeds. Maybe she pulls the data or someone pulls it for her? Why are you asking?"

"Exploring different possibilities." I pulled a second cutting board out of the cupboard, grabbed a knife, and chopped the tomatoes. "Alice spends a lot of money." I filled Brad in on my visit to Bryce and Alice.

"I told you. She's done well with her investments. Plus, I pay her well."

"I paid a visit to Ted's ex."

"Oh?"

"Long story. She was super chatty. She said he is ruthless when it comes to the competition and you should watch your back."

He looked up from the chopping board and asked, "You think he might be behind all this?"

"Maybe. I definitely feel like I'm getting closer to breaking the case."

"God, I hope so." After he set the knife down, he walked over and kissed my neck. "Why don't you slip into your bathing suit? I'll feed Duke his dinner while you change."

Duke howled an "I love you" at the mention of dinner.

I looked forward to an evening of relaxation by the pool and Brad's kisses.

Chapter 26

Apollo observed Atlas at the outdoor shooting-range, as he hit the bullseye once again. As Apollo had laid awake last night, he'd come up with an idea. He cleared his throat, "Good shot."

"Thanks, boss. Atlas set the rifle down. "You wanted to see me?"

"How is the shooting practice coming along?"

"Excellent, still sharp as ever," he beamed.

"Keep at it. You're going to need it." He stepped closer. "I thought of a new way to permanently distract that woman." He lowered his voice. "Follow me. We need a bit more privacy."

Atlas followed Apollo to a bench where they'd be able to hear each other over the gunshots of the four other shooters practicing at the range.

Apollo leaned forward and said, "I have an important mission for you. No one but you and I must know. Understood?"

"Yes, sir." Atlas's chest swelled.

"You," Apollo paused for effect, "are the Chosen One." A grin spread across his face. "Listen very carefully."

"Yes, sir." Atlas beamed.

"Take one of the vehicles and drive to San Diego immediately. Bring your rifle, ammo, and whatever supplies you need. There's an Ironman competition this Saturday. Scope out the track and find out where people gather to watch the race. Then find a concealed area where you could take a clean shot at someone."

"Who's the target?" Atlas could barely contain his excitement.

"Liz Adams. She'll most likely be on the sidelines cheering for her boyfriend," he sneered. "The best time to get a clean shot is during the running part of the race when everyone will be focused on the athletes."

"You got it, boss."

"We will have no communication. I can't have this traced back to our organization. As soon as you complete the task, haul your ass back here." Apollo narrowed his eyes. "And if you fail, cross the border into Mexico and await further instruction."

"I won't fail."

"Good. Any questions?"

"No, sir." Atlas didn't want to ask how he'd receive further instructions. He was determined to succeed.

"Then I suggest you get started."

~ * ~

Peanut ducked behind the brush as soon as he heard his name. He peered through the branches and watched as Cosmo dangled a fifty-dollar bill in front of his neighbor at the homeless camp along the river. While Cosmo fished for information on Peanut's whereabouts, the man gave him just enough to earn the cash.

Panicked, Peanut darted into a nearby drainpipe and exited out the other side. Time to head to the railroad tracks. He'd hop a freighter and get the heck out of here until the coast cleared. He knew Apollo would be ticked he'd left the compound, but he'd no idea that he'd go to this length to find him. He wished he could let that nice cop know what was going on. No time. He needed to skedaddle and fast.

Peanut stopped at a convenience store and bought some snacks to take along before he headed to the tracks. He scoped out the train and crawled into an empty boxcar. While he munched on a stick of beef jerky, he waited for the train to depart. He wondered where Rumor was. If she were here with him, they'd make up stories and pretend they were on a fancy vacation. He fingered the card the cop gave him. Maybe when the train stopped, he'd find a way to call her to see if she'd found Rumor. After all, she promised.

Chapter 27

The next day, I met Sam at the entrance to my property. A ponytail hung out the back of her neon yellow ball cap. Dressed in black shorts and a jacket that matched her hat, she was the sunshine missing on this foggy morning. I wore my bright orange windbreaker with an air horn tucked in the side pocket.

"We look like citrus fruit," I joked. I set the thermos of coffee on the hood of the Rover and hung the bag with Styrofoam cups and bottles of water on the front fender. "Brad says hi. He sent fortification."

"Awesome." She helped herself to a cup of joe.

While I handed her a stack of no trespassing signs and a staple gun, I asked, "Do we need to do this any certain way?"

"Definitely need to post a couple at the entrance. And then space them along the fence about every three hundred feet."

"Do you think we have enough?" This could take all day. I wished I'd asked Brad to help.

"Probably not." She thought for a moment. "Why don't you take the side to the left of the gate, and I'll take the right? When you get down to your last fifteen signs, go to the end and start to work your way backward. We'll need to post signs down by the beach since that seems to be where he enters the property."

"There's an area in the interior with a picnic table and a porta-potty. Do you think we should post any there?"

"Probably not a bad idea. Let's check with each other every hour on the hour and see how we're doing."

"OK. Let's do this." I positioned a sign on the left side of the gate and punched the staple gun.

After an hour of stapling, my hand was sore, and before too long I'd need to pee. I placed a call to Sam. "How ya' doing?"

"Making progress. You?"

"I need a pee break. You wanna meet me at the gate and drive down to the porta-potty? I can show you the beach."

"Girl, just drop your pants and go."

"Never, I might get my shorts wet."

"Wuss."

"A girl's gotta have her standards." I harrumphed.

She relented, "OK, I could use a break too."

Sam was waiting for me when I arrived back at the entrance. "You realize we'll waste at least half an hour to save your precious shorts." She smirked and then added, "Let's take my car, it'll be quicker."

I made a beeline for the toilet as soon as I hopped out of her car.

When I finished, Sam was sitting on top of the picnic table inspecting her nails.

"Better?" she asked.

"Much. You need to go?"

"No. Unlike some of us, I have skills."

"Ha. C'mon, I'll show you the beach." My phone buzzed as we walked down the trail.

"I can't find him anywhere," Brad's voice sounded panicked.

"Can't find who?" I asked.

"Duke! I let him out back and then went to the study to check email."

"I'm sure he's fine," I replied, attempting to reassure myself. "Did you try calling out 'treat'?"

"Yes. I'm telling you, Liz. I checked the beach. I checked the guesthouse. I checked everywhere."

Oh my God. My stomach sank.

Sam took one look at my face and mouthed, "What's wrong?"

I held up one finger in response to her question then turned my attention back to Brad. "Wait. You have cameras. Have you checked the footage?" I asked.

"Good idea. I didn't think of that."

"I'll be there as soon as I can."

My eyes watered as I told Sam what had happened. "My dog's gone missing. This project's going to have to wait."

"Oh no," she gasped. Grabbing my hands, she squeezed them. "I'll go with you. Between the three of us, we'll find him."

Once we packed up and were in our cars, Sam hit the sirens. I followed her as we peeled down the freeway.

I jumped out of the Rover and ran into the house calling for Brad. No answer. I flew out the back door. "Brad," I screeched.

"Over here." He emerged from a clump of trees that bordered the property. "The security footage shows him entering here." He pointed at the paw prints on the soft ground. "About halfway in, some shoe prints join the tracks."

Sam joined us. "Maybe it's some kid who thought he found a lost dog. Liz, do you have a recent photo of Duke?"

I looked at her like she was crazy. "Of course." Most of the pictures on my phone were of my dog, including my screensaver.

"Why don't you and Brad print up some lost dog posters? I'll take some imprints of the tracks." She continued, "Then the three of us can post the flyers and canvass the neighborhood. Is he chipped?"

"Yes."

She grabbed my arm and looked me in the eyes. "That works in our favor. We're going to find him."

Although I was somewhat comforted by Sam's take-charge attitude, I was unsettled. I had no reason to believe any foul play was involved, but my dog was still missing. After two hours of searching, we returned to the house without him. I felt sick to my stomach. An envelope addressed to me sat on the front doorstep. I bent down to pick it up.

"Wait." Sam grabbed my arm. She slipped on latex gloves, opened the envelope, and pulled out the note. I noticed the typed letter was on standard paper. Sam read the letter out loud before she bagged it.

"Quit butting in where you don't belong. Drop everything and make arrangements to permanently return to South Carolina by Monday five p.m. Leave copies of the evidence of your travel plans in locker 101 in the women's locker room at Forever Fit on Carmel Rancho Blvd. If everything checks out, you'll receive further instructions to get your dog back. No tricks or you'll never see him again."

In all my years as a private investigator, no one had ever threatened Duke. I pushed the front door open and strode toward the study silently fuming. Brad followed while Sam secured the evidence.

I positioned myself behind the desk and said, "Pull up the surveillance footage. Let's see if we can find who left this."

Halfway through the time we'd been searching the neighborhood, a black Honda with no plates pulled into the driveway. A person dressed in a black hoodie exited the driver's side. It appeared to be a man, mostly because of the height, but it could be a woman. A bandanna and dark sunglasses shielded the person's face. He walked up the steps to the front door and dropped the envelope on the welcome mat.

Sam entered the room. We replayed the three minutes over and over and searched for any identifiers on the car or the person's clothes. "Can you email the clip to me?" she asked.

"You got it," Brad replied.

"Any idea who might have done this?" she added.

I shook my head. "Butting in where you don't belong . . . what does that mean? It could be Ted. It could be the identity thief. It could be Apollo. It could be anyone." I groaned in frustration and then narrowed my eyes. "No one threatens my dog."

Brad turned to Sam. "Where do we go from here?"

"I think you should cooperate," Sam said. "At least while I run the prints to see if we can determine who's behind this."

"Cooperate? You can't be serious. We need to catch the perp." My voice raised an octave in fury.

"I agree with Sam," Brad said. "When we get Duke back, we'll know who did it."

I looked back and forth between Sam and Brad and considered their advice. "True. As long as we craft the right statements . . ." I trailed off.

"What? The dog talks?" Sam shook her head.

For a moment, I debated telling her. "You can't tell anyone."

"Scout's honor." She held up three fingers. "What the hell are you talking about?"

I told her about my dog's lie-detecting abilities.

"Are you serious?"

Brad and I responded in unison, "Yes."

"Man. We could use a dog like that on the force." She wrapped her arms around me. "It's going to be OK. I'll try to get prints from the note, and I'll see what I can determine from the footprints."

When Sam left, I couldn't contain my anxiety. I needed to talk to someone from home. I stepped outside and phoned Lou. "Duke's been kidnapped!" I said before he could say hello. Without taking a breath, I spilled the details.

"Wait, doll. Slow down. Someone took your dog?"

"Yes," I replied through gritted teeth. I summarized the contents of the ransom note.

"Poor baby." I wasn't sure if he meant me or Duke. Lou asked, "They don't want money? They only want you to drop whatever and come back to Charleston?"

"Yes. Then supposedly that will be the end of it."

"That's crazy. Any idea who did it?"

"Nothing solid." I filled him in on Sam and the steps she was taking to find the culprit.

"Have you asked Peg for help?"

"*What?*"

"You know at first I didn't believe all that woo-woo stuff about the hummingbird at the cemetery when Peg died, but who knows? Maybe she could help find him. Or at least calm your nerves. It wouldn't hurt."

Not long after Peg's death, I'd seen a hummingbird when I'd visited her grave site. Maybe Lou was right. "Not a bad idea," I promised to keep Lou posted on the latest and said goodbye. As I lifted my face to the sky, I asked Peg to give me a sign.

Thirty seconds later, a hummingbird whizzed past my right ear.

"Is Duke going to be OK?"

The bird returned and flew past my left ear. I took the return as a yes.

Brad called out the back door for me.

"I'm here," I replied.

He draped his arm around my shoulder and said, "I guess we should start making those flight plans."

~ * ~

The next day, I was up at five a.m. I couldn't sleep. With the absence of Duke in the bedroom, and last night's empty dog bowl, I felt like I was living a bad dream. Brad had tossed and turned but had finally fallen asleep. I threw on a sweatshirt and shorts and tiptoed into the kitchen. Once I'd made a cup of hot tea for fortification, I headed to the guesthouse. Last night we'd printed off the confirmed flight arrangements. We planned on placing the documents in the locker at four p.m. I was determined to discover the culprit before then.

Brad had copied me on the email he sent Sam. I opened the video and replayed the footage. I panned and zoomed in on the images. Whoever it was appeared to be about six feet tall. I couldn't make out any facial features. The hoodie, sunglasses, and bandanna concealed ninety percent of the face. I could see a portion of the neck. There was no tattoo. That ruled out 'Dice Man.' The bandanna was solid black, and there was no logo on the hoodie. Same with the sweatpants. Both garments made it difficult to tell how much the perp weighed. The tennis shoes bore the Nike logo. The sweatshirt sleeves hid half of his hands, which were covered in latex gloves. Was he working alone or in cahoots with someone else? Even though the perp had been good at concealing his identity, the entire operation had an amateur vibe to it.

As I zoomed in on the vehicle, I tried to determine if a dog or anyone else was in the car. The windows were too darkly tinted to see anything inside. The passenger side door had a dent. Other than that, there were no distinguishing marks.

"Duke, who took you?" I groaned. At the bottom of the whiteboard, I listed the possibilities. Ted was the right height. Come to think of it, so were Bryce and Dr. Stanistreet. I added their names. Mitch was too short, and Chandler was about half a foot taller. If Alice had anything to do with it, she'd hired someone.

Online, I found a rental car agency that delivered. I ordered a nondescript gray sedan. On second thought, I ordered two. We needed to divide and conquer. The vehicles would arrive by nine a.m. Time to wake Brad from his slumber.

Over breakfast smoothies, I filled Brad in on my plan. "Whoever has him will have to let him out to do his business." I sipped on the protein shake. Not bad. "I'll stake out Ted and you can stake out Bryce. Do you have any high-powered binoculars or a camera with a decent zoom lens?"

Brad shook his head. "By the way, I already called Alice. I told her I wasn't feeling well and to clear my calendar for the day."

In my quest to get Duke back, I nearly forgot Brad was the CEO of a major corporation. My heart swelled at his commitment to find my dog. "We can swing by the sheriff's office on our way out. I'm sure Sam will loan you something. If not, I'll use my camera, and you can take my binoculars."

"Good idea. We can get an update from her while we're there." He wiped the smoothie mustache from his upper lip with a napkin and continued, "What if they're watching us?"

"My gut says no. This feels like an amateur operation to me. I don't think they have the manpower. But we need to watch for tails."

"How?"

"Follow my lead. When we head out, we'll take a couple of sharp turns. Trust me, we'll be able to tell."

"And if we are being followed?"

"I'll have to think of a Plan B." I stood and rinsed out my empty glass.

*

I took several sharp left and right turns as I watched the rearview mirror to make sure that Brad kept up. Once I'd confirmed no one was following us, we drove straight to Sam's office. I had texted her before we left to let her know we were coming. We rushed into the station.

Sam was waiting for us at the front desk. "Don't you both look cute in your Johnny Cash black?" She led the way down the hall to her office. "Follow me."

I took off my sunglasses, placed them on the rim of the ball cap, and followed her.

When we entered the room she said, "I don't have a lot of news for you. But I do have some updates. Have a seat." A half-eaten donut was perched next to her computer on a napkin. She pushed the box of remaining donuts toward me. "Help yourselves."

"No can do." Brad patted his stomach. "Triathlon coming up."

I perused the box of pure sugar and also declined.

"I have good news and bad news. There were two prints on the letter. Neither one matched anything in the national database."

"What's the good news?" I asked.

"We were able to determine that the shoe is a tennis shoe, Nike brand, men's size eleven."

I wondered how we could find out Bryce and Ted's shoe sizes. "I noticed the Nikes when I reviewed the footage."

Sam continued, "I've personally placed calls with all the area animal shelters. They'll call me if Duke shows up. One of my deputies is contacting local vets." She bit into her donut and chased it with a swig of coffee.

Local vets. I said a silent prayer for his safety. "I can't thank you enough."

"You have any further thoughts on who might've taken him?"

I filled Sam in on my morning's efforts and our plan to stake out Bryce and Ted. If our efforts were fruitless, I'd place the documents in the locker and pray my dog would be returned to me shortly afterward. "I feel like this is an amateur effort, what do you think?"

"I tend to agree, but you both need to be careful. Call me if you need me, and I expect full updates."

"Yes, ma'am."

Sam walked around the desk and gave each of us a hug. She looked me in the eye and said, "You're going to get your dog back."

My eyes watered. I nodded in response.

Chapter 28

Back in the rented vehicles, Brad and I headed our separate ways. I'd given him a hand-drawn map of Bryce's apartment complex and marked a couple of spots I considered ideal for a stakeout.

Ted's place would be more difficult. My first hurdle was the gated country club community. When I pulled up to the guard gate, I claimed I was interested in becoming a member. The guard jotted down my name and my vehicle details and then handed me a visitor's pass. As I drove toward Ted's street, I admired the architecture of the large homes. A Mediterranean-style house with a curved entryway caught my attention. Oak trees flanked the front. Mounds of orange zinnias surrounded the trunks. Cherry red camellia blooms abounded on the bushes. A sign in the front yard boasted "Yard of the Month."

The second hurdle was Ted's house. The place was surrounded by a wrought-iron gate. I had trouble finding a spot where I could approach without being noticed. While I continued down the street, an idea occurred to me. I followed the signs to the country club, parked the car, and bribed one of the cart staff for a golf cart. I claimed I wanted to tour the course. The young man had no problem pocketing the hundred-dollar bill.

On my earlier drive-by, I'd noticed a clump of trees behind Ted's house which had to be where his property met the course. I pulled up a map of the community on my phone and located the hole Ted's property bordered. After I parked the cart, I placed my phone on silent and waited until the golfers headed to the next tee box. Once the coast was clear, I ducked into the clump of trees. I found the perfect spot with a view of Ted's backyard where I was semi-protected from stray golf balls.

What appeared to be the family room had floor-to-ceiling windows. The backyard had an infinity pool and a practice putting green. I zoomed in with my camera lens and searched for signs of my dog. When I settled the lens on the bay window, I spotted Ted at a table reading the newspaper. I didn't see the Russells. Ted stood and stretched his arms toward the ceiling. Dressed in belted shorts and a tucked-in polo, he looked ready for a tee time. The back door opened, and he stepped out, putter in hand, the Russells in tow. No Duke.

While the dogs did their business, he practiced his putts. They sniffed along the fence line and then started yapping my way.

"Boys, when will you learn you can't catch those damn squirrels from here?" Ted muttered loud enough for me to hear. "Let's go inside and get a treat before you piss off the golfers." The Russells responded to the word treat and followed Ted back inside.

I breathed a sigh of relief and shot off a quick text to Brad.

> How's it going?
>> Nothing yet. No sign of Bryce or Duke. You?
> I spotted Ted with his dogs. No Duke.
>> How long do we wait?
> As long as it takes. Looks like Ted is heading out to play golf. I may be able to get closer.

> Be careful!
>
> I will :)

As soon as I hit send, a call came in. "Hello," I whispered.

"Are you the owner of a black lab named Duke? This number was on his name tag." The woman on the other end asked.

Hallelujah. I couldn't care less if anyone heard me now. I raised my voice a few notches. "Yes. How'd you find him?"

"He showed up on my doorstep. I have a golden retriever, and she started barking. As soon as I saw the tag, I called. He's a beautiful dog."

"Thank you." I breathed a small sigh of relief before I asked, "Is he OK?"

"He's fine. He and Belle are playing tug of war in the backyard." She rattled off her address.

I located a pen, asked her to repeat it, and scribbled the information on my arm. "I can't thank you enough. I'll be there as soon as I can."

"No rush, I'm here until two. Then I leave to pick up my kids from school."

I gathered my gear and rushed toward the cart. As I pressed the pedal down to the floor, I called Brad. "Duke's been found," I squealed with glee.

"That's great news. Is he OK?"

"He's fine." I filled Brad in on the details and read the address off my arm. "If you get there before me, will you please wait?"

"Of course."

"Thank you. She's expecting me, and I need to be there to greet him."

I couldn't wait to hug my dog.

While I raced toward the clubhouse as fast as the cart would go, I spotted Ted on the driving range. "Toodle loo, Ted." I fluttered my fingers in the air.

~ * ~

As soon as he saw me, Brad hopped out of the car. We strode hand in hand toward the mission-style home made of white stucco. The dark wooden door was framed by two long, glass windows. A barking frenzy began as black and yellow balls of fur charged the entry. "I guess there's no reason to ring the bell." I chuckled as tears of relief rolled down my cheeks.

A petite Asian woman opened the door and attempted to hold the dogs back. "You must be Liz. Please come in."

Once inside, I dropped to the ground and nuzzled my dog's neck.

"I can't imagine Belle being lost. I'm Amy." She extended a hand to Brad.

"Brad. We're both so grateful to you. You have no idea how much." Brad pulled out his wallet and a couple of hundred-dollar bills.

"Oh, no. Please, no money." She waved her hands in the air. "Maybe he can come back and play with Belle sometime. She adores him."

He bounced up and down on his front paws. I stood and wiped the tears off my cheeks. Belle joined in on the fun and circled Brad and me. "She's a beautiful dog. I'm sure he'd love to come play." He barked in reply, his tail swishing in the air.

Brad bent over and massaged Duke's ears. "Good to see you, buddy."

Duke howled, "I love you."

"Oh my gosh. Did he just say I love you?"

I nodded.

"That is so adorable."

After we said our goodbyes, my dog dashed out the front door before I could put a leash on him. "Duke, stop," I screamed.

He stopped, circled in place, and barked.

"I think he wants us to follow him," Brad said.

I rushed over and snapped the leash to his collar. He immediately lunged forward pulling me along. "I think you're right," I called out over my shoulder.

I sprinted and followed his lead to a gray house two doors down. He sat on the doorstep and barked. The home badly needed a fresh coat of paint. An older woman in a wheelchair answered the door.

"Oh, Duke. You're back."

"Who is it, Mom?" a woman's voice called out. She joined her mom at the front door.

"Zelda?" Brad and I said in unison. He edged his way inside, "What's going on here? You'd better explain."

Zelda's face sank. She hung her head and mumbled, "I'm sorry."

Her mom asked, "Why are you sorry, hon?"

"Nothing, Mom. Let's sit in the kitchen. Follow me." She wheeled her mom into the kitchen. "Ok if I get Mom settled on the back porch?"

"OK by me." I sensed she didn't want her mother to hear whatever confession was about to occur. I shot off a quick text to Sam.

> Found Duke. He's OK. Can you send someone over here?

I typed in the address and pressed send.

Sam's reply arrived seconds later.

> Good news! Be right there.

After Zelda settled her mom at a table on the porch with a glass of orange juice and her crossword puzzle, she plopped in the chair next to Brad. "My mom has MS. She needs nursing care during the week while I'm at work."

"I know your mom has MS, but what does this have to do with you taking Duke?" Brad asked.

"Please let me explain, I'm truly sorry, Brad. You've always been good to me, but insurance only covers a small portion of the nursing care. It's expensive." Tears rolled down her cheeks and splashed on the rubber place mat as she hung her head. "Bryce promised me no one would get hurt. It was supposed to be an easy way to earn some extra money." She raised her head and shrugged, "I mean . . . the people were already dead." After blowing her nose into a napkin, she continued, "And then *she* started poking around." She glared at me. "I only agreed to help take the dog to get *her* to go back to Charleston. I'd never be a part of something where an animal or a person got hurt."

I clenched my fists under the table. "You took my dog from the house?" She didn't fit the image I'd seen on the camera.

She explained that Bryce had been the one to kidnap him. He'd lured the dog from the backyard with treats and then brought him to Zelda's in his cousin's car. After he'd dropped Duke off, he'd returned and placed the note on the front doorstep.

Exasperated, I allowed Brad to take charge of the questioning. Slowly, he coaxed the full story of the identity thefts out of her. Once a client had been reported deceased, she'd pulled the victim's details and passed the information along to Bryce. She didn't know what happened afterward, but each victim earned her a seven thousand dollar payout. Brad looked crestfallen.

My phone rang.

"I'm here," Sam said on the other end.

I stood. "You know we're going to have to turn this over to the authorities."

Zelda's hands flew to her heart. "What about my mom?"

"I'll take care of your mom," Brad responded. "If you'd come to me in the beginning, I would've helped you out."

My heart melted. I added, "If you fully cooperate with the authorities, there's a chance you'll receive a lighter sentence."

I left the room to let Sam in and asked her to stop at the kitchen doorway where she'd be out of sight of Zelda's mother.

As soon as Zelda spotted her, her mouth formed an O, and she started to shake.

"Where can I find the number for the nurse?" I asked.

She pointed to a notebook on a desk. "Will you please also call my cousin and ask him to come stay with her?"

I nodded and handed her a pen and paper, and she wrote down the name and number.

"I'm sorry, Brad," she repeated. Hunched over, she stood and shuffled toward the doorway. Sam delayed cuffing her until they were at the front door.

~ * ~

While we waited for the pizza to arrive, Brad paced the living room. Duke snored softly on the couch. He was exhausted.

Brad ran his fingers through his sandy brown hair. "I can't believe Zelda was involved."

"Sounds like she was desperate to help her mom."

"At least it wasn't Alice." He sighed. "I knew Zelda's mom had health issues, but I'd no idea it was that bad. All she had to do was talk to me or Tim." He sat on the couch next to Duke and roused him from his slumber. "And to kidnap a dog? I never would have expected that. She seemed like such a kind person." He shook his head while he stroked my dog's back.

I walked behind the sofa and massaged his neck and shoulders. "I expect Bryce was the mastermind. Zelda strikes me as a follower."

On the way back to Brad's, we'd placed a call to Tim to let him know what had happened. Tim and Brad decided to tell the staff that Zelda was out on personal leave. As far as Bryce was concerned, a new auditor would show up with no explanation. Tim wondered if he should switch firms. I promised to deliver my final report this week, so we could tie up that loose end with the employees. Sam would take care of letting the Monterey police know the perps had been caught.

As the knots in Brad's neck melted, I continued, "Maybe Zelda wasn't comfortable coming to you or Tim. Have you considered hiring an HR manager?"

"Not really." He thought for a moment as he scratched Duke's belly. He purred with contentment. "It might not be a bad idea. We've grown large enough that it makes sense."

"Just a suggestion, but how about putting a hotline in place?"

"A hotline?"

"You know, an anonymous line anyone can call to report something suspicious or a violation of policy. An HR manager can coordinate the set-up and then help investigate the claims." I sighed, "I don't know if having it in place would've prevented this situation, but it's an extra measure of protection." The doorbell rang, and Duke dashed for the door.

"Enough shop talk." Brad stood to retrieve our food. "Let's enjoy our pizza and relax. We both deserve it."

I couldn't agree more.

Chapter 29

Atlas referred to the map of the race he'd printed off in the motel's business center. He wore a Hawaiian shirt, shorts, and sunglasses to blend in with the other tourists. As he walked along the street where the running part of the competition would take place, he scouted out the neighboring buildings and trees. A parking garage on the east side of the street looked promising. He climbed the four flights of stairs to the top and studied the elevated roof above the exposed stairwell. If he lay on his belly, the structure should be high enough to conceal his presence. Tonight when no one was around, he'd shimmy up and take a look. He was determined to succeed.

While he walked through the garage and pretended to search for his car, he scoped the space for cameras. The only ones he found were by the entrance and exit gates. Yep, this was as good a place as any. He wished he could call Apollo and tell him. Tomorrow, he'd study the weather and further case the area. He prayed for light winds.

~ * ~

Cosmo pounded the streets that bordered the shopping center. He pawed off a twenty and handed the money to a man who claimed that he'd seen Peanut camped out under a bridge by the river. The end of the hunt pulsed in his veins. He was getting closer. As he navigated the rocks along the riverbank, he spotted a blue plastic makeshift tent underneath a bridge. When he discovered a young woman in her twenties, he cursed. She'd claimed the spot a month ago. She didn't know anything about a man named Peanut. He continued, determined to find him. Had to be a different bridge. Peanut was around here. Somewhere.

~ * ~

Apollo reviewed the Mission Abort plans he kept locked in the safe. If Atlas failed, he might have to enact them. At some point, he'd have to brief the Chosen Few in case the worst happened. As he chewed on his fingernails, he read the documents three times. Confident every detail had been contemplated, he placed them back in the safe. Then he called Cosmo. "You found him yet?"

"Not yet, boss. I got some good leads. Several people saw him in the area."

"I hope you find him and fast." Apollo hung up the phone.

He crossed the grounds to the chapel, knelt in the front pew, and meditated. Too much was happening at once. He needed to clear his head. As much as he wanted to visit the sacred ground, he was hesitant to do so after the cop's last visit. He couldn't wait to get that wretched PI out of the picture.

Chapter 30

Duke led the way up the steps of the private jet. I trusted Tim, but I wasn't ready to leave my dog behind after the kidnapping. We were booked into a pet-friendly resort close to San Diego, and I'd found a doggie daycare close by where he could stay while I cheered Brad on in the race.

The last few days had been hectic. While Brad upped his training schedule for the triathlon, I'd rushed to complete the final report and then reviewed my recommendations with Tim. We'd presented the results and next steps to the staff over a series of employee meetings, wrapping up the last one yesterday.

When they arrested Bryce, he'd spilled the details of the scheme. The FBI was now involved. Sam seemed relieved to hand the case over. I'd spent hours with two agents filling them in on my discoveries and passing on my notes. Brad worried about what would happen to Zelda. The outcome was out of our hands.

As I settled into the plush leather seats, I smiled. I looked forward to enjoying the sights of San Diego. Brad leaned down and kissed me before he sat in his chair. Duke thumped his tail between us. Next week I'd be back in Charleston. I etched Brad's features into my brain. When the plane taxied down the runway, he gripped the armrests so hard his knuckles turned white. "You OK?"

"I will be. The take-offs and landings are the toughest." He glanced up and looked at me with those aquamarine eyes. The butterflies fluttered in my stomach, and my heart dropped. Although I was ready to be back home, we'd spent nearly three weeks together. I was going to miss him.

My heart skipped a beat. I would miss this man, *a lot*.

~ * ~

After we'd checked into the hotel, we took Duke to Dog Beach. As he pranced in the water and played with a pair of golden retrievers, the knots in my neck eased. A cool breeze blew off the Pacific Ocean. Sunshine warmed my arms. I grabbed the Frisbee out of Brad's hand, ran down the beach, and flung it his way. Duke and his new friends joined us in the game. An hour later, exhausted, we called it quits. Once I'd hosed my dog off, we rinsed the sand off our feet and then searched for a spot to eat. I was starving.

"When we're finished eating, I'll show you a couple of good spots to watch the running part of the race."

Fingers interlocked, I squeezed his hand. "OK. I'm so glad I stayed to watch you."

"Me too." He emphasized his words with a kiss.

We found a dog-friendly restaurant with a patio that faced the beach. The server brought a bowl of water for my dog and asked us for our drink orders.

"Water for me," Brad replied.

"I'll take a glass of your house chardonnay."

"So, tell me about the race," I asked as I studied the menu.

"It's a half Ironman Triathlon. It's not as long as a typical race. San Diego is the first race I ever competed in. We'll start with a one-point two-mile swim in the Pacific. Normally I'd get here earlier to practice, but with everything that's been going on...," he trailed off.

"Sounds grueling."

"Can be. For the swim, it depends on the waves. They were very choppy in my first race. I panicked, but I was determined to finish for my sister."

I waited for him to continue.

"My times were terrible. But, I made it across the finish line. I've improved every year since then."

Duke emptied his water bowl and lay next to my chair. I admired Brad's determination and dedication. "How many compete?"

He rubbed his chin. "This year, I think about three thousand."

"Will there be a lot of spectators?" I set the menu down.

"Yeah. I'll show you a spot towards the end that tends to be less crowded."

The waitress placed our drinks on the table. "Are you ready to order?"

I nodded, "I'll take the crab cake sandwich. Can I get onion rings instead of fries?"

"Of course. Good choice. And you?" She batted her eyelashes at Brad.

"Rib eye, medium with steamed veggies." He handed her the menus.

"Either of you want a salad?"

"No thanks," we replied in unison.

Brad continued his description of the race. After the swim, there'd be a fifty-six-mile bike ride followed by a thirteen-point one-mile run. The bike ride wound through the military base. He entertained me with stories of last year's race where he'd placed second in his age group, edging out Chandler by eight seconds.

The server arrived with our food. Brad cut off bites of rib eye and placed them on a napkin for Duke.

"What's the hardest part of the course?"

"If it's windy, definitely the biking. Doesn't look like it'll be too bad this year."

My phone pinged with an email from Lawson. "That's odd," I commented. With all the events of the last few days, I'd forgotten I'd asked Lawson to track the shipping addresses.

"What?"

"Lawson found the address where the drugs are being shipped." I stared at my phone in disbelief. "Mission Apollo."

"That is strange. You think Apollo is a drug dealer?" Duke pawed Brad's leg for another bite of meat.

I shrugged. "I dunno. I forwarded the email to Sam. I did my part. It's up to the cops and the FBI to figure the rest out."

As we ate our meals and people-watched, I shared stories of Duke as a puppy, and Brad described other competitions. The breeze blew through my hair as I savored the sweet crab sandwich and the crispy onion rings. I wondered if Peg knew how blissfully happy I was at this moment.

After our late lunch, we walked to where the finish line for the running portion of the race would be. The finish line banner stretched over the street. "Most people will gather down toward the end. If you can, find a spot somewhere in here . . ." He gestured to the sidewalk on the east side of the street. "There won't be as big of a crowd, and you should be able to watch me finish."

"You gonna win?" I poked him in the ribs.

"You betcha." He grinned. "I think it's time to get back to the hotel for a crucial part of my training." As he kissed me long and deep, I had no doubt what he meant.

~ * ~

Brad left sometime before dawn for the competition. The previous night he'd checked his bike in and attended a briefing meeting while I'd stocked up on Ironman gear in the gift shop. I planned to leave by nine, drop Duke off at doggie daycare, and then be positioned in place no later than ten-thirty. My nerves hummed in excitement for Brad's big day.

The sky was a cloudless blue, and the breeze light. I was glad I'd worn my bright orange windbreaker over my new Ironman t-shirt. The temperature was in the sixties. I squeezed my way between a group of people who wore matching shirts with "Team Jack" emblazoned across the front and a family holding signs that read '*Go, Sara! You can do it!*' The crowd was much denser than I'd expected.

I made small talk with a woman who turned out to be Sara's mother. This was Sara's first race. She'd been training for a year. As I picked up conversations from some of the members of Team Jack, I discovered Jack had placed first in his age bracket two years ago. The group would move toward the finish line as soon as they spotted him. Good. I stood on tiptoes and searched for the lead runners. No one was in sight, yet.

Chapter 31

The planets were aligned. Atlas couldn't believe his luck. Yesterday, while he rested his feet on a park bench, he'd spotted the woman and her boyfriend. He'd wandered close enough to catch part of their conversation and then pieced together that this area was where she planned to watch the race. Not far from the parking garage. To make his mission even easier, she'd shown up today in a bright orange jacket, making her an easy target. How could he miss? He'd confirmed it was her when he zoomed in with the high-powered lens.

Adrenaline pumped through his veins. He'd risen early to avoid race security. The concrete roof on top of the staircase was cool on his belly. Even though he'd been positioned in place since three a.m., he didn't feel a bit tired. He adjusted the rifle and peered through the eyeglass. The crowd around the woman in the orange jacket was a little less dense. He'd have to wait for the right moment to pull the trigger. He was ready for the kill. Liz Adams was going down.

~ * ~

Apollo couldn't resist. He wanted one last look around the sacred ground in case he needed to implement Mission Abort. The fog dissipated as he parked the car along the bordering fence and began to walk toward the beach. On his approach, he spotted that pesky cop stapling 'No Trespassing' signs on the opposite side. He halted, dashed behind a tree, and peered around the trunk. The cop grabbed her gear, edged her way past the fence, and on to the beach. His heart pounded when she paused in front of the cavern, switched on her flashlight, and then ducked inside. Apollo waited an agonizing thirty minutes before she emerged holding a phone to her ear.

His stomach sank as he feared the worst. He darted back to his car and sped back to the compound. On his way, he called Cosmo and commanded him to return. Pronto.

Back in his office, he switched the four televisions on the wall to various news stations. He fired up his computer and pulled up the livestream of the triathlon. Once Cosmo had arrived, he'd summoned the Chosen Few and briefed them on the plans to eliminate the private investigator and preserve the sacred ground. If his plan failed, they would need to implement Mission Abort.

He handed each of them a copy of the document. Looks of shock registered on each of their faces as they read the papers.

"Any questions?" Apollo's jaw was set.

No one dared ask as all eyes locked on to the computer screen.

Chapter 32

I spotted the runners sprinting down the track and searched for Brad's number. When I located Brad, I grabbed Sara's mom's shoulder and pointed. "That's my boyfriend." He was about twenty runners behind Jack. Team Jack hooped and hollered and headed for the finish line. I moved forward in the empty space Team Jack had vacated. While I waved my arms I shouted, "Go, Brad!"

He was about a yard from me when a force shoved me to the side. I tripped and banged my knee on the concrete. Then all chaos broke loose. I watched as Brad fell to the ground in slow motion.

~ * ~

Atlas had a clear shot at the target. He honed in with his scope and squeezed the trigger. He stared in disbelief when she moved to the right as if propelled by some unseen force. While he watched her fall, he hoped the bullet struck. Within seconds, she was back on her feet racing toward one of the runners. Havoc ensued as the crowd scattered in every direction.

He peered through the lens and confirmed he'd missed Liz and struck the runner. His heartbeat quickened while police and security scanned the landscape for his location. He'd no time for a second shot. News vans and reporters filled the areas vacated by the crowd. He left the rifle behind, shimmied down the roof, and sprinted down the stairs. He tore off his black hoodie and gloves, tossed them into a waste bin, and stepped into the streets in an Ironman t-shirt. He looked like any other spectator. After he'd donned his sunglasses, he strode toward the spot where he'd parked his car and prayed he'd make it to the border.

~ * ~

Apollo watched Atlas's failure unfold as the race streamed on his computer. The Chosen Few stood by his side, while the television screens flashed with breaking news about a sniper shooting in San Diego. The culprit was still at large.

Apollo collapsed in his chair and shook his head in disbelief. Wife number two gathered up the papers and shredded them. Other than the sound of the shredder, the room was silent. Apollo nodded toward Cosmo, "Gather the Members in the chapel."

With somber faces, they proceeded one by one to implement Mission Abort.

~ * ~

While I screamed Brad's name, I pushed over the flimsy fabric and metal barrier that separated the spectators from the participants. People scattered in all directions. I ran toward Brad. Crowd control was useless. The limited security focused on locating the shooter. I prayed Brad was alright.

"Oh my God. Are you OK?" Blood streamed down his right calf.

"What happened?" He appeared dazed.

"I think you've been shot." I pulled a pocketknife out of my tote, tore off my windbreaker, and lifted the new t-shirt over my head. While I attempted to shield my exposed bra from reporters' cameras, I sliced into the fabric and tied the makeshift tourniquet above the wound. Satisfied the bleeding had slowed I slipped my jacket back on, scanned the area, and prayed a medic would show up. Brad grabbed my hand and stood.

"What are you doing?" I asked as blood seeped down his leg. "You need to be still until help gets here."

"I'm finishing the race." His jaw was set. He hobbled forward.

After a few seconds of disbelief, I made up my mind. I rushed to his side and grabbed his right elbow. We shuffled together toward the finish line. His breathing was labored, and he was drenched in sweat. After we crossed, he turned to me, grabbed my shoulders, and kissed me. As the cameras and video cameras recorded the scene, he said, "Liz Adams, I love you," before he collapsed to the ground.

The medics placed Brad on a stretcher, and I followed them to the ambulance. The EMTs allowed me to ride with them to the hospital. I clutched Brad's hand, as they started an IV. His eyes fluttered open.

"I finished," he grinned.

"Brad O'Connor, I love you too, but don't ever pull that crap again."

~ * ~

Brad was lucky. The fabric fence had slowed the high-velocity shot. Although the bullet tore through the back of his calf, it had missed the bone and there was minimal damage to the muscles. He needed stitches and lots of rest. The biggest worry was infection from any fibers or dirt the doctor was unable to remove from the wound. He'd be discharged later that evening. Brad was ready to summon the plane, but I'd convinced him to stay in the hotel one more night.

While the doctor stitched Brad up, I Ubered back to the rental car. Duke was excited to see me when I picked him up from doggie daycare. On the ride back to the hotel, he seemed to sense my anxiety as he placed his head in my lap. The latest news reported the shooter hadn't been caught. Was it a random shooting or targeted? Was one of us the target? I recalled the unseen force that pushed me. If that hadn't happened, would I have been hit?

Once in the safety of the hotel room, I breathed a deep sigh and checked my phone. I had two missed calls from Sam and ten missed calls from my parents. I returned Sam's call first.

"Liz, thanks for calling me back. I need you to agree to a search of your land."

"Have you seen the news?" I asked.

"What news? I've been too busy trying to line up resources to gather evidence from your property."

"Evidence?" I had no clue what she meant.

Sam filled me in on how she'd gone to post the rest of the no trespassing signs and discovered the cavern. She'd navigated the narrow passageway into a large opening where she'd discovered over a hundred dead bodies wrapped in cloth and stacked on top of each other. Horrified, she'd run back out, called for backup, and then secured the scene.

"Oh my God. Do you think Apollo's behind this?" My stomach churned.

"Most likely. When will you be back?"

"Tomorrow." The whole thing was beyond creepy.

"Why did you ask if I'd seen the news?"

"Brad and I are semi-famous," I announced in a caustic tone. "We're all over the local news." I told her about the hell my day had been.

"Girl, you've had a week."

"Tell me about it."

"I hope Brad recovers soon. Tell him I say hello."

As soon as I hung up, my phone pinged with a text from my neighbor, Lou.

> Is Brad OK? I heard he was shot.

How had the news already made it to Charleston?

> He's going to be fine. How did you find out?

Hon, you've gone viral. The video clip of Brad confessing his love and then collapsing is all over the web.

Will you let the neighbors know everything is OK? Jenny too? I'll call when I can.

Great. Now I knew why I had ten missed calls from my parents. I called my mom's cell.

"I've been trying to reach you," she scolded. "We've both been worried sick." Her voice caught. "We saw you on the news." She put her phone on speaker.

"How are you, and how's your boyfriend?" The elevated tone in my dad's voice conveyed worry.

"We're fine." Duke yipped in the background. My dog was right. I was not fine. My nerves were beyond frazzled. "He's getting stitched up now. I'm about to head back to the hospital to pick him up."

"Did they catch the shooter?" Dad asked. Mom was silent. Not a good sign.

"Not yet, but I'm sure they will. I heard on the news the police found the rifle."

"I didn't even know you had a boyfriend." I imagined the pout on my mom's face. "I thought you were visiting a friend."

My dad interrupted, "When do we get to meet him?"

"Soon. I promise." I pledged to send them an update once Brad was released, and we said our goodbyes.

As I snatched the car keys off the nightstand and left to pick up Brad, my mind churned. Was I ready to introduce him to my parents? They'd been heartbroken when Sawyer and I divorced. What if Brad and I didn't make it? And was I honestly imagining a future break-up when I'd just confessed my love? Sam was right. It'd been a week.

~ * ~

Back in Brad's hospital room, I flipped on the TV and channel surfed as we awaited his release. He was groggy from pain meds but in good spirits. I paused the channel when the announcer said "Mission Apollo" as breaking news flashed along the bottom of the screen.

"Mission Apollo, a refuge for homeless men and women, just suffered a series of explosions." The reporter went on to describe what had happened at the compound. I gingerly sat on the end of the bed and stared as the camera panned to a neighboring home where a reporter held a microphone. I turned and looked at Brad. "Can you believe this?" He shook his head.

"Neighbors thought there was an earthquake," the reporter continued. The camera angle broadened and an older man and woman appeared on the screen. "Our whole house shook," the man said.

"It was terrifying," the woman added. The screen switched to an aerial view of flaming buildings surrounded by fire trucks. Smoke swirled as orange and red blazes roared toward the sky. The perimeter of the property was being doused in water to prevent a wildfire. The announcer concluded, "There are expected to be no survivors."

I filled Brad in on what I'd learned from Sam. "I guess we'll never find out if he was dealing drugs," I added.

Brad shook his head. "Those poor people."

Chapter 33

Peanut hopped off the train in King City. He found a secluded spot to bathe in the river and rinse his clothes. As soon as his clothes dried, he headed into town and searched for something to eat. While he strolled through the streets of downtown, he paused and peered into a bar. The place was empty. The roasted peanuts in barrels beckoned to him. He entered and found a bar stool where he could watch the front door and then splurged on a Coke. As he opened and peeled the nuts, his eyes darted between the baseball game and the news. He nearly choked when he saw Mission Apollo blow up in flames on the screen. "Holy smokes," he exclaimed.

"Yeah, looks pretty bad," the bartender said as he dried off a glass. "They're saying no survivors."

Peanut dabbed at his eyes with a napkin. All those people and their kids. He thought about Charlie, his bunkmate, and that sweet child, Sally, who'd held his hand once during worship. Sure, it was a weird place, but nobody deserved to be blown to bits. He shook his head as he struggled to absorb the news.

~ * ~

Atlas hadn't been so clever after all. The cops discovered the black hoodie and latex gloves in the trash bin and lifted his prints. They'd issued a statewide all-points bulletin. In his haste to get away, he'd gotten caught speeding. He'd refused to answer questions until they connected the vehicle to Mission Apollo and shared the footage of its demise. Crestfallen, he'd confessed everything, including how the compound had a warehouse that distributed black market drugs across the country and how Apollo selectively sold the identities of the deceased to a cartel. Apollo had always said it was a way for the departed to live on, and the extra cash from both efforts further fueled the Mission's expansion. It was supposed to be for the good of the mission. Atlas shook his head.

It had all been for naught.

Chapter 34

Tomorrow, I'd return to Charleston. Brad was out back grilling a feast of tenderloin steaks, lobster, and vegetables. As I tossed the salad, the doorbell rang. I put down the tongs and answered the door.

"Hi, Sam."

"Came to say goodbye. But first, I have someone I want you to meet. Duke too."

Curious, I followed her out front with my dog in tow. Sam opened her car door and an enormous bloodhound bounded out. "Meet Judge."

"Oh my gosh, he's adorable. Those ears. Those wrinkles." I rubbed Judge's back while he and Duke sniffed each other. "Is he yours?"

"Yup. He's one of the dogs rescued from the Mission."

Although all the buildings had perished, the kennels had remained unscathed. "Have they adopted all the rescues out yet?"

"Every single one." She smiled. "I need to get back to the station. Promise you'll keep in touch?"

"Promise. I need you to teach me a few more dance moves." I did a little jig.

"Yeah, we're going to have to work on that." She stepped around Judge and hugged me.

~*~

I joined Brad outside. Duke wagged his tail as he searched for lizards in the container pots that bordered the pool. I sighed. I would miss this. "Sam stopped by. She has a new pet."

"Oh?"

"One of the rescues from the compound, a bloodhound, Judge. And good news. All of the dogs got adopted out."

"Great!"

As I watched him flip the steaks, I reflected on all that had happened. Brad's wound was healing nicely. The shooter had confessed I'd been the target and Apollo was behind the whole mess. He'd also spilled the story behind the graveyard in the cavern.

Sam's team was working the property in conjunction with the FBI. She claimed between the identity theft and mass murder investigations there were more agents than tourists in Carmel. I wondered if I'd ever be able to sell the property, or if it would remain forever tainted. My thoughts were interrupted by the ring of my phone.

"Only in California," I commented as I ended the call.

He set the spatula to the side and faced me. "Who was that?"

"The real estate agent. A production company wants to rent the property after the FBI clears out. They want to make a movie based on Apollo's story." I shook my head in disbelief.

"Get out."

Honestly, I couldn't make this stuff up. "They want to put down a hundred-thousand-dollar deposit to secure the deal. My guy's sending me the paperwork tomorrow."

Brad turned his attention back to the grill. "Maybe you can take a well-deserved extended vacation."

"That'd be nice," I replied as I watched a hummingbird feast on nectar from a clump of California Fuchsia. While the sun began its descent over the ocean, I recalled the unseen force that pushed me aside. I could have lost my life. Why did I continue to guard my heart? Hadn't Peg's death already taught me life was short? I silently forgave Sawyer and myself for our failed marriage.

Brad turned back toward me and studied my face. "Whatcha thinking about?"

I returned to the moment and shared what had happened at the race. "Do you think it was Peg?" She had left letters for each person who was mentioned in her will. In her letter to me, she'd promised to be my guardian angel.

"It's possible," he replied.

A hummingbird darted toward me and hovered next to my face before flying away. "Wow."

"Speaking of wows . . ." He popped open a bottle of champagne and poured each of us a glass.

I stood and accepted the flute of bubbly. "Cheers."

"Not yet."

He cued up a song on his phone. Savage Garden's, "I Knew I Loved You." After he'd extracted a box from his pocket, he knelt in front of me on his good leg. As the lyrics spilled from his phone, he removed a ring and placed it on my left hand. "Liz Adams, will you marry me?"

"But where will we live?" I sputtered.

He sighed, "I may sell the company. Some investors approached Tim while we were gone."

"You'd sell the company?"

"Yes . . . After everything that happened . . . I want a real family. I want you."

My heart melted as I exhaled. "Yes."

~ * ~

On my way back to Charleston, I texted Jenny with the news and then called my parents. Although my mom was miffed I was engaged to a man she'd never met, she couldn't wait to plan the wedding. Brad and I were still debating over the date. He wanted to get married on Valentine's Day. I thought that was kind of cheesy. At least we'd agreed to a schedule for visiting each other barring some unforeseen event. He'd be in Charleston next week.

My neighbors ambushed me as soon as Duke and I returned home. As Lou, Gwen, Cassie, Maria, and Linda gathered in my living room, I described Brad's proposal. "Well of course I said yes." I grinned.

Lou grabbed my hand and examined the ring. "Girl, that's a rock."

The emerald-cut diamond set in platinum glittered in the light. "It was his mother's." I smiled. "It couldn't be more perfect. She never wore her good jewelry when she traveled." I clutched the ring close to my chest.

Cassie put her hands on her hips, "Ladies, sounds like we have a wedding to plan." Duke joined in on the excitement with a woof.

Lou chimed in, "What do you mean ladies? I'm in on this too. After all, I am a designer." He took a bow.

Uh-oh. I was in trouble.

Acknowledgments

My mission is to deliver a good read to the reader and benefit a larger community. A portion of the proceeds from this book is donated to Texas Sporting Breed Rescue where we adopted our Labrador, Eve, and other organizations that help homeless pets. A big thank you to my readers, I couldn't exist without you. If you enjoyed the story, I would sincerely appreciate a rating or review.

It indeed takes a village to create a book. Many thanks to Carrie Kerskie, identity theft, fraud, and privacy consultant, for graciously sharing her expertise with me. An additional shout-out to our friend and triathlete, Kent Mayes, who shared his experience with triathlons. And last but not least, thank you to Herman Bennett, cyber security expert who shared his vast knowledge of the information technology world. Any errors are entirely my own.

A big thank you to my beta readers, Mary Ellen, Mary Pat, Eileen, Susan, Sandy, Sarah, Jeff, and John. Many thanks to all who supported me along the way, most especially my greatest cheerleader, my husband. A shout-out to Whitney and Jimmy for lending their marketing expertise. Thank you also to my parents, my aqua fit helpers, my author and artist friends, my cover designer, my interior formatter, and my editors.

Keep turning the page for Liz's recipes and a sneak peek at Cayman Conundrum.

All the best,
Stacy Wilder

Liz's Lasagna Casserole

Serves 8-10

Ingredients for sauce:
2 cans (14.5 ounce) petite diced tomatoes drained

2 large garlic cloves, grated	2 heaping teaspoons Italian seasoning
1/2 teaspoon sugar	1 can (15 ounce) tomato sauce
1 pinch oregano	1/4 cup water
1 can (12 ounce) tomato paste	5 tablespoons finely chopped red onion
1 pound hamburger meat	1/4 teaspoon fennel

Combine all ingredients except for the red onion, meat, and fennel in a saucepan. Add salt and pepper to taste. Bring to a simmer and then turn the heat down.

On medium-high, heat a drizzle of olive oil in a skillet. Saute red onion for thirty seconds and then add one pound hamburger meat and fennel. Add salt and pepper to taste. Once the meat is brown, drain and add to sauce. Cover and simmer on low heat for at least thirty minutes stirring occasionally. An hour is better. Turn off the heat, uncover and allow the sauce to cool down.
Ingredients for the casserole:

1 15 ounce container of ricotta cheese	8 ounces of grated mozzarella cheese
1 1/2 cups grated parmesan cheese	9 ounce package of oven-ready lasagna noodles

Divide the sauce into two bowls. Grease the bottom of a 9x13 inch pan. Layer noodles on bottom and then pour in one bowl of sauce. Sprinkle 3/4 cup of the parmesan cheese on top. Dollop 8 heaping tablespoons of ricotta cheese evenly across casserole. Press down to spread. Finish with one cup of mozzarella sprinkling heavier on the edges. Repeat. Cover with foil and allow to sit in the refrigerator for at least an hour.

When ready to bake, preheat oven to 400 degrees. Bake covered for thirty minutes. Uncover and bake for fifteen more minutes, then broil for approximately two minutes. Watch to ensure the top turns slightly brown and doesn't burn. Remove from oven and allow to stand for fifteen minutes before cutting. Serve with Caesar salad and garlic bread. Enjoy!

Brad's Birthday Cake

This recipe is compliments of Piece and Love Cakery, Houston, TX. The company is owned by two sisters, Gigi Welling Nitzberg and Kerry Stovall. Their mission is to make beautiful things that taste like childhood, baking and making moments special. Many thanks to Gigi and Kerry for this delicious cake recipe!

Ingredients for cake:

5 large eggs

1 1/2 cups granulated sugar

1 ¼ teaspoons almond extract

1 ½ teaspoons pure vanilla extract

3/4 cup almond flour

2 cups unbleached all-purpose flour

3/4 teaspoon salt

1 ½ teaspoon baking powder

1/2 cup milk

12 tablespoons unsalted butter, melted and cooled

Ingredients for frosting:

4 sticks unsalted butter (room temperature)

6 cups powdered sugar

1/4 cup meringue powder

2 teaspoons vanilla

1/2 teaspoon almond extract

1/4 teaspoon salt

2 tablespoons cherry juice concentrate (use the juice from a jar of maraschino cherries)

Ingredients for filling:
2 cups cherry pie filling
3 tablespoons hot water

For the cake: Preheat oven to 325 degrees. Grease three six-inch round cake pans and line the bottoms with parchment. Grease the parchment. In a large bowl, combine the eggs and sugar. Beat on high speed with whisk attachment until thick and lemon-colored. Slow the mixer and add the melted butter and extracts. In a separate bowl, whisk together the flours, salt, and baking powder. Add to the egg mixture in three additions, alternating with the milk. Scrape the bowl and beat for another 30 seconds. Divide the batter into the three pans, about two cups per pan. Bake for 34-37 minutes, until the edges start to pull away from the sides and the center springs back when lightly touched. Cool cakes in the pans on a cooling rack.

For the frosting: In a bowl, with hand mixer or stand mixer, mix softened butter with meringue powder and powdered sugar. When combined, add extracts and salt. Add cherry juice 1 tablespoon at a time, mixing well after each one.

For the filling: Add hot water to pie filling. Strain juice from the cherries into a bowl separating the cherries and the juice. Set aside.

Layering the cake: Brush ¼ cup cherry filling juice on bottom layer of cake. Spread ¾ to 1 cup of frosting, pushing it toward the outer edge and creating a shallow well. Put 1/3 cup of the reserved cherries in the well (making a dam around the edge will keep the filling from pushing out and dripping out the sides). Repeat with the next layer. Frost the top layer, then continue with frosting around the sides. If the frosting seems thin, put it in the fridge for five minutes to let it stiffen. The cake can be chilled to set the frosting, but let it come to room temperature before serving.

Enjoy!

Author's note – I used two 8 ½ inch cake pans, extending the cooking time 15 minutes. Gigi gave me a great tip – Listen to the cake. If it's sizzling, it's not done yet. The cake is cooked when it barely sizzles. The recipe would also be great as cupcakes, skipping the filling. Delicious!

Liz's Caesar Salad

Ingredients:

Romaine lettuce, washed and torn into bite-size pieces
Parmesan cheese
Garlic croutons
Fresh ground pepper
Dressing (Liz credits her neighbor Linda with the recipe):
3 tablespoons ranch dip (Liz uses Marzetti brand)
1 tablespoon Dijon mustard
2 teaspoons Worcestershire sauce
Salt and pepper to taste

Combine ingredients for dressing in a small bowl. Slowly add water until the dressing reaches desired consistency (Liz adds very little water). Toss lettuce with dressing and place on salad plates. Garnish with cheese, croutons, and fresh pepper.

Enjoy!

Brad's Conundrum Cocktail

This recipe is compliments of the team at Hugh O'Connor's Irish Pub, Houston, TX. Hugh O'Connor's served the cocktail during the book launch party for Charleston Conundrum. Thank you, Hugh O'Connor's team for creating the cocktail and allowing me to share this recipe.

Ingredients:

1 ounce orange vodka
.75 ounces vodka
.75 ounces St. Germaine
.25 ounces Malibu rum
.25 ounces lemon juice
.25 ounces lavender syrup (add more to taste)
Splash of grenadine

Pour ingredients into a martini shaker. Mix, add ice. Shake multiple times. Strain and pour in a martini glass. Garnish with a lemon wedge. Enjoy!

Linda's Famous Jalapeno Poppers

Take Linda's cue and put together a smorgasbord of nibbly bits for your next book club meeting.

Ingredients:

1 dozen fresh jalapeno peppers
1 8 ounce package cream cheese, softened
3 green onions, whites, and green parts finely chopped
12 thin slices uncooked bacon (for extra kick, use Hormel's jalapeno bacon)
1 garlic clove minced
Salt and pepper to taste

Preheat oven to 400 degrees. Wash produce. Half jalapenos, scooping out and discarding seeds. Dice onions. In a bowl, combine cream cheese, garlic, and onions. Season with salt and pepper. Fill each half of the peppers with about two teaspoons of the cheese mixture. Placing two halves together, wrap the pepper with bacon. Line a baking sheet with aluminum foil and top with a wire rack. Place the poppers on the wire rack and bake for 25 minutes, then broil for another 2 minutes or until bacon is crisp. Let cool for a few minutes before serving and then serve warm. Enjoy!

The Carmel Conundrum Playlist:

1. "Hotel California," The Eagles (thanks to Barry Edick for the song suggestion)
2. "Only The Good Die Young," Billy Joel
3. "California Dreamin,'" The Mamas & the Papas (thanks to Mary Ellen Hendricks for the song suggestion)
4. "Glitter in the Air," P!nk
5. "King of the Road," Roger Miller
6. "California Girls," The Beach Boys (thanks to Barry Edick and Mary Ellen Hendricks for the song suggestion)
7. "Celebration," Kool & The Gang
8. "Take My Breath Away," Berlin
9. "Hit the Road Jack," Ray Charles
10. "(Sittin' On) the Dock of the Bay," Otis Redding
11. "Life is a Highway," Rascal Flatts
12. "Bad Day," Daniel Powter
13. "Girls Just Want to Have Fun," Cyndi Lauper
14. "I Knew I Loved You," Savage Garden

A sneak peek at....Cayman Conundrum

The words flowed from Tim's fingertips onto the page. He stood and stretched his arms toward the ceiling. As he rubbed his newly acquired goatee and watched the turquoise waves softly lap against the white sand, he reflected on last night's conversation with his informant at the bar. After the man, he only knew as Jax, had consumed three shots of tequila, he'd spilled secrets about the money laundering business on the island.

Since the identity thefts from his former company, MultiPoint Protection Services, Tim had been obsessed with the connection between black market drugs and money laundering. After he and his former partner, Brad, sold the company, he'd moved to Grand Cayman and took another step toward fulfilling his dream of becoming a full-time author. Previously, he'd had a few short stories published, but this was his first attempt at a full-length novel. Fictionalizing the real-life details, he hoped the new thriller wasn't too close to the truth. Tim saved the document onto the jump drive and locked the device in the desk drawer. His phone pinged with a text.

Why haven't you called or messaged me?

He put the phone down and opened the back door to let his new dog, Snooper, inside. A salty breeze drifted through the doorway. He shook his head and wondered why he'd ever gotten involved with the former beauty pageant queen. At first, they'd had fun. He was instantly attracted to her almond-shaped hazel eyes and deep-throated laugh. Becky was funny, charming, and stunning. He'd met her when he volunteered with the island's animal rescue group where he adopted Snooper. They shared a desire to help homeless pets.

A month into the relationship, she became jealous, possessive, and controlling. He regretted inviting her to join him as his plus-one for Brad and Liz's upcoming wedding in Charleston, S.C. His shoulders slumped. He wished he could find a soulmate like his friend and former business partner, Brad, had found in Liz.

Snooper bounded toward Tim's cat, Irish. The black and white Labrador and cocker spaniel mix was a ball of energy at six months old. Irish hissed stopping the puppy in his tracks. Tim chuckled and then turned and picked up his phone.

> Sorry, busy working on the book. Meet up for drinks at five at The Deck? We can talk about travel plans.

He hit send, placed the device down, and walked toward the kitchen to feed his pets without waiting for a reply.